P9-DMF-143

THE YELLOW FEATHER MYSTERY

THE famous young detectives Frank and Joe Hardy are caught up in a dangerous web of intrigue when they agree to help Greg Woodson search for his grandfather's missing will. Greg feels sure that he is the rightful heir to his grandfather's property, including Woodson Academy, but no trace of a will can be found.

Greg's grandfather had promised to tell him about "Yellow Feather" shortly before he died. Who or what can Yellow Feather be? And where does Henry Kurt, the temporary headmaster of Woodson Academy, fit in? He insists that he is to inherit the school. Moreover, Kurt claims to have been threatened by Yellow Feather!

Frank and Joe risk their lives several times before they solve the mystery of Yellow Feather and trap a sinister criminal who will stop at nothing—even murder—to satisfy his greed for money.

Joe pulled himself and the boy up

The Hardy Boys Mystery Stories®

THE
YELLOW FEATHER
MYSTERY

BY

FRANKLIN W. DIXON

ST. JOHN THE BAPTIST PARISH LIBRARY
2920 NEW HIGHWAY 51
LAPLACE, LOUISIANA 70068

GROSSET & DUNLAP
Publishers • New York
A member of The Putnam & Grosset Group

ST. JOHN THE BAPTIST PARISH LIBRARY
LAPLACE LOUISIANA 70068

Copyright © 1971, 1953, by Simon & Schuster, Inc. All rights reserved.
Published by Grosset & Dunlap, Inc., a member of The Putnam & Grosset
Group, New York. Published simultaneously in Canada. Printed in the U.S.A.
THE HARDY BOYS® is a registered trademark of Simon & Schuster, Inc.
GROSSET & DUNLAP is a trademark of Grosset & Dunlap, Inc.
Library of Congress Catalog Card Number: 78-158746 ISBN 0-448-08933-5
ISBN 13: 978-0-448-08933-1
5 7 9 10 8 6 4

CONTENTS

CHAPTER I

A Strange Request

SKATING against the stiff evening wind, Frank and Joe Hardy streaked across the frozen surface of Willow River toward Woodson Academy. The bright winter moon was rising beyond the buildings on their right along the riverbank.

"Why do you suppose Gregory Woodson phoned us to meet him at the school boathouse?" Joe asked.

"Just before the connection was broken, Greg said he feared that someone might overhear us in the dormitory," Frank told his brother. "I guess what he's going to tell us must be top secret."

"It sure sounds so," Joe remarked as the boys approached the meeting place. "Well, he ought to be here. It's five-thirty."

Dark-haired Frank Hardy, eighteen, and his blond brother, a year younger, were known in

Bayport, where they lived, as clever detectives. Although they were still high school students, they often helped their father, a nationally famous sleuth, solve baffling cases. Occasionally they were asked to solve a mystery on their own, like the present one.

When the boys reached the boathouse raft, the building was pitch black and the silence intense. Suddenly a youthful voice called quietly:

"Come straight across the float, fellows. I'm right in front of you!"

"Is that you, Woodson?" Frank asked.

"Yes, it is. You're the Hardys?"

"That's right."

As the boys walked forward on their skates, a tall, slender young man moved out of the shadows. The Hardys judged him to be about twenty-two.

"I'm sorry we were cut off when you phoned," Frank began. "You want us to help you solve a mystery?"

"Yes. My grandfather, Elias Woodson, was headmaster and owner of the Academy until his recent death. It's about the inheritance I'm supposed to receive that I'd like to talk to you."

Both Hardy boys immediately warmed up to the pleasant young man and Joe said, "Our father's an alumnus of the Academy and knew your grandfather well. I'm sure Dad would want us to help you."

"Thanks," Woodson responded. "I'm glad you'll take the case—you might call it the mystery of the Yellow Feather."

"Yellow Feather?" Joe repeated.

"I'll explain in a moment," Woodson replied. "I have a key to the boathouse. Let's go inside out of the wind and I'll show you a clue I brought along."

As the boys were about to enter the building, a wild scream out on the river arrested their attention.

"Look there!" Joe cried.

A short distance down the shore several students were skating near a large bonfire. Close by a large black hole yawned in the ice. Joe caught sight of a young boy trying to crawl back from the thin-surfaced area at the edge of it.

Joe did not wait. Like a flash he was off across the ice, with Frank and Greg trailing him. As Joe approached, the youngster shrieked in terror, crashed through the ice, and disappeared. There were cries of horror from his companions.

Without hesitation Joe slid into the dark water. As Greg Woodson and Frank looked on, ready to help, he rose to the surface with the struggling boy.

"Hold on!" Frank cried.

He had spotted a long log near the bonfire. Grabbing one end of it, he asked Greg to help him. Together they laid the log across the thin ice and the hole. While they held it, Joe pulled himself and the young skater up on it and slowly they made their way to a safe spot on firm ice.

Immediately the rescued twelve-year-old began to shake from the shock of the icy water. His friends crowded around in awe and fright, explaining to the Hardys that they had been playing snap-the-whip when their end player, Skinny Mason, had been flung off the firm ice.

"You okay, Skinny?" one of the players asked.

"I-I g-guess so."

Frank whipped off his heavy leather jacket and wrapped it around the shivering boy.

"Th-thanks," Skinny quavered. "I'll b-be all r-right now." He looked gratefully at Joe and added, "I'll never forget that you s-saved my l-life!"

"Come on. We'd better get you both to the school," Greg urged.

An older boy skated up, saying that he would take charge of Skinny. As he moved off with the youngster, Joe turned to Greg.

"Is there any place we can go where I can dry my clothes? I want to hear the rest of your story."

Greg thought a moment. "I've got it—the caretaker's cottage. Nobody will be there at this hour. The door's always open and I know the Teevans well. They've been here a long time."

When the boys reached the snow-covered riverbank they removed their skates and hurried through a patch of woods to the Teevan house. A low light shone inside. As Greg opened the door and invited them to enter, he remarked that Mrs. Teevan was the school cook.

A few minutes later the three were seated before an open fire. Joe had wrapped Mr. Teevan's bathrobe about him while Greg put his clothes in the dryer. Then young Woodson made hot cocoa for all of them.

As Frank sipped the steaming drink, he said, "Tell us your story, Greg."

"The night before Grandfather's death I received a phone call from him at Myles College, where I'm a student. He explained that his health was failing rapidly, and he wanted to tell me about the Yellow Feather.

"I never did find out what he meant," the young man continued. "Grandfather suddenly became ill and hung up. The next day I received a call from Henry Kurt, the assistant headmaster, that my grandfather had died."

"That's too bad," Frank said. "How long ago was this?"

"Several weeks," Greg replied. "So far no will has been found. But Grandfather told me that he had willed me his entire estate."

Frank raised his eyebrows. "Have you contacted his lawyer?"

"Yes. Grandfather obviously never consulted him in this matter."

"Has a thorough search been made?" Joe inquired.

"Sure. I even tested all the walls at the school for secret panels and hidden closets. But now I have a new worry. Since I've been here searching, I've received several mysterious phone calls and a couple of unsigned letters warning me to leave Woodson Academy. I think the person is the Yellow Feather!"

The Hardys looked at each other, perplexed.

"It's a mighty queer name for anyone unless he's an Indian," Joe commented. "Have you any clues to his identity?"

"Just a couple of days after Grandfather's death, I received a peculiar letter. Grandfather had addressed the envelope—I'm sure of that, even though the ink was nearly washed off. Inside was a sheet of white paper with the name *Hardy* printed in the top left corner."

"Yes?" Frank prodded, startled to hear that his own family might be involved in the mystery.

"That was the only writing on the sheet," Greg explained. "But below the name was something most unusual—a group of small rectangular cutouts arranged horizontally. Here, I'll show it to you."

Greg crossed the room to where his jacket hung over a chair. He ran his hands through the pockets, at first slowly, then with frantic speed. At last he wheeled about, his face ash white.

"The paper—and the envelope—I've lost them!"

At the Hardys' suggestion Greg Woodson made a search of all his pockets for the missing envelope. But it was of no avail.

"That piece of paper might be the key to the mystery of the Yellow Feather!" he said.

"Perhaps you dropped the envelope when we were rescuing Skinny," Joe suggested.

Greg snapped his fingers. "Of course. It must have slipped out then."

"Let's take a look," Frank proposed.

Joe's clothes were now completely dry, so he quickly donned them. Greg borrowed flashlights from the kitchen closet, then the three boys grabbed their skates and hurried from the cottage. At the river's edge they sat down to put on their skating shoes. As Greg knotted a broken lace, he said, "I'd hoped to become Grandfather's assistant here after I graduate from college in June. Then when he died, I figured on running the school myself."

"But until a will is found you can't do that, I suppose," Frank said.

"That's right. And it won't be easy to run the school even then. For the last few years, it has been a financial struggle to keep the Academy going."

"Dad has mentioned that the enrollment's fallen off," Joe spoke up.

"But with certain new ideas I have, I believe it would pick up again," Greg answered. Then he added, "I'm afraid the Yellow Feather is in some way responsible for the missing will. That's why it's so important to find him."

By this time all three had started down the river. Fanning out with the borrowed flashlights, they searched from the boathouse all the way to the scene of Skinny Mason's mishap.

"No envelope here," Joe called.

There were negative responses from Frank in the middle and Greg on the other side.

Refusing to give up, they scanned the river-bank, thinking the wind might have blown the letter up on the shore. No luck!

Frank was about to suggest that he and Joe start for home and return in the morning when they heard the noise of a motor.

"Where's that coming from?" Greg asked.

The buzzing sound seemed to be coming closer. As the boys peered toward a bend in the river, waving their flashlights, Frank shouted, "Hey, look out!"

With a shove he sent Greg and Joe sprawling to one side. As he did, a shadowy bulk bore down on them and whisked past in the darkness.

"Wow!" Joe exclaimed. "What kind of ice-boat was that?"

Before anyone could answer, Frank gave another cry of warning.

A shadowy bulk bore down on them

"Here it comes back!"

But this time the iceboat was moving slowly. Just before it reached them it scraped to a complete stop.

"Hi, fellows! Thought I recognized your voices."

"Chet Morton!" the Hardys cried out.

"What kind of gimmick is that?" Joe asked.

"It's a cross between a bobsled and an iceboat," said Chet as he hopped from the weird contraption. "I just finished putting it together a little while ago."

The heavy-set boy was a loyal friend who had faced danger with the Hardys in many of their exciting adventures ever since he had helped them unravel their first mystery, *The Tower Treasure.*

With a sheepish grin Chet said, "I sure didn't mean to come so close to you fellows, but I couldn't see very far ahead. Besides, the rudder's not working right."

Frank introduced pug-nosed, freckle-faced Chet to Greg, then examined the strange-looking craft with his flashlight.

"No sail," he observed. "But you certainly were moving along, Chet. Say—what's this back here—a propeller?" Chet nodded.

"Almost like a catamaran," Joe commented, "but for travel on ice. It's a pretty swell idea."

Proudly Chet admitted to being the inventor.

"Not only for ice," he corrected Joe, "but for snow. It has interchangeable runners."

Greg was impressed and said so.

"It works fine," Chet told him. "That is, I was moving along pretty well until some guy on skates crossed right in front of me. I almost turned myself inside out to avoid hitting him."

Chet pointed to the rudder, which was bent out of position.

"And then he had the nerve to bawl me out," the boy complained. "I thought he'd shake his goatee right off onto the ice."

Greg started. "You say he wore a goatee? Was he a man in his late thirties?" Chet nodded, and Greg went on, "That must have been Henry Kurt, the assistant headmaster I was telling you fellows about. The court appointed him to be in charge of the school until the year's over."

"He looked more like an absent-minded professor to me than a headmaster," Chet remarked. "Skating along, trying to read some piece of paper by flashlight, instead of watching where he was going."

Greg and the Hardys looked at one another. Could Kurt have picked up the missing letter?

Frank and Joe decided they would certainly try to find out the next day. After a few minutes' further conversation, Greg excused himself to return to the Academy, saying he would see the boys in the morning.

"Sure thing," they agreed.

After Greg had left, Frank said, "Let's get this contraption started and head back to Bayport."

"Yes, crank her up, Chet," Joe demanded. "You can tow us all the way to town—and a late dinner."

But when their stout friend attempted to spin the flywheel of the small motor which ran the craft's propeller, there was no response. Grunting from the exertion, Chet tried again and again.

"Something's wrong!" he wailed. "It won't catch! Well," he added with a resigned sigh, "I guess you fellows will have to tow *me* home."

"What!" Joe protested. "We can't drag that thing five miles to Bayport. It would take all night."

Frank offered the only possible solution. "Biff Hooper's folks have a summer place up here, you know. We can pull your gimmick over to their dock, Chet, and tie it up for tonight. Tomorrow you can come back and do a repair job."

"Okay," Chet agreed. "But you'll have to help me."

It took only a few minutes to find the Hooper cabin. After Chet had lashed his craft to the dock, he put on the skates he had brought along and the trio headed for Bayport.

It was well past the usual dinner hour at the

Hardy home when Frank and Joe trotted up the front steps. Mrs. Hardy met them at the door.

"I'm glad you're home!" said their mother, a slim, pretty woman, who had been watching anxiously for her sons. "Your dinner's in the oven."

Another voice, pleasant but firm, broke in. "You're lucky we saved you something. How come you boys are so late?"

The speaker was their father's sister, who lived with the Hardys. Each time her nephews got involved in a new case, she predicted dire consequences. But despite their Aunt Gertrude's constant chiding about the risks they ran, the boys were extremely fond of her.

Before Frank and Joe could explain the reason for being late for dinner, a deep male voice boomed out, "Hi, boys. Good thing you're here. I want to talk to you before I catch a plane."

Fenton Hardy, their tall, dark-haired father, smiled broadly as he came downstairs. He led them into the dining room, and while Aunt Gertrude served them roast lamb and vegetables, the young sleuths reported their adventure.

When they had finished, Mr. Hardy grinned. He reached into his pocket and drew out a white piece of paper.

"Have a look at this," he said and held it up.

In the upper left-hand corner the name *Hardy*

had been printed by hand. Below it were a series of rectangular cutouts!

Both boys stared dumbfounded, then cried out, "Where'd that come from?"

"Henry Kurt, the headmaster of Woodson Academy, brought it to me a little while ago."

"What!" the boys shouted in astonishment.

"Kurt," Mr. Hardy went on, "wants *me* to solve the mystery of the Yellow Feather!"

CHAPTER II

A Three-cornered Puzzle

"KURT asked you to solve the mystery of the Yellow Feather?" Frank gasped.

"Yes," Mr. Hardy replied. "He left here just a short time before you arrived. He had a pair of skates tucked under his arm—must have skated down from the school."

Joe asked breathlessly, "Did he say where he got the paper?"

The detective shook his head. "No, that never came up. I told him I was leaving town for a week—that I'd help him when I returned. He gave me the sheet of paper and urged that I get on the case as soon as possible."

"Same thing Greg asked us," Frank said.

Mr. Hardy smiled. "I see no reason why we couldn't combine our sleuthing. You can work on the case while I'm away."

The boys nodded.

"Before I leave, though," the detective went on, "I'll get off a telegram to the FBI, asking if they have any listing of a criminal known as the Yellow Feather."

"In the meantime, we can try to find out who he is," Frank said.

"And also the significance of the paper with the cutouts," Joe added.

"But remember," their father said, "the courts will take care of the legal aspects of the inheritance, pending the appearance of a will. You won't have to worry about that."

It was decided that the following day Frank and Joe would inform Greg Woodson and Henry Kurt of the Hardys' decision to work together.

Next morning, as the boys sped along in their convertible with Frank at the wheel, they discussed what the reaction would be to their announcement about the Hardys combining their sleuthing.

"I wonder how Greg and Kurt will take the news," Joe remarked.

"It's my guess that Greg will be a good sport about it," Frank replied, "but Kurt might not like the idea."

"We know Greg's story," said Joe. "Let's tackle Kurt first and see what he has to say."

Reaching the site of Woodson Academy, Frank turned into the winding driveway. Ahead of them in the snow-covered landscape stood a long colonial-type brick building partially covered with ivy. From it rose a circular bell tower.

Frank parked in front of the main entrance and the boys hopped out. A student just coming out of the building gave directions to the headmaster's office.

The door was opened by a slender, graying man, who carried himself very erect, with an almost military bearing. His dark eyes were keen and he wore a well-trimmed pointed goatee.

As soon as introductions had been exchanged, Henry Kurt said crisply, "Have you boys brought me a message from your father?"

"Yes. He asked us to speak to you and Greg Woodson together," Frank replied.

"Greg and me? Together?"

"Yes," Frank answered. "We find you're both interested in the same mystery."

A trace of annoyance crossed the man's face. "Umph! Well, if that's what your father wants . . . certainly. Just a moment."

Kurt sent a messenger to the Academy's guest room to summon Greg. Then he said, "I understand that your father is an alumnus of our school."

"He is," Frank replied. "And he's very much concerned about what happens to Woodson Academy."

"Naturally," Kurt remarked. "That's why I believe we can work together."

It took only a few minutes for Greg Woodson to join them. The young man looked puzzled at seeing the Hardys in the headmaster's office but greeted them pleasantly. Frank, as spokesman, explained the boys' mission. Both Kurt and Greg showed an immediate antagonism toward each other.

To break the tension, Greg said, "It's all right with me if Frank and Joe work for both of us. The quicker this mystery is solved the better."

Kurt surveyed the young detectives icily, but finally he said in a flat tone, "I suppose if your father thinks you're capable of handling an affair as important as this I'll have to trust his judgment."

"Dad knows what he's doing, Mr. Kurt," Frank replied. "Now, would you mind clearing up one point?"

"What is it?"

"We've been wondering where you got the sheet of paper you left with Dad last night—the one with the rectangular cutouts."

"It was given to me by Elias Woodson just before he died. He didn't have time to tell me what the cutouts meant. So I took it to your father to decipher."

"Why did you wait so long?" Joe asked.

"I've been busy reorganizing the school," Kurt reminded them. "I want to talk to you boys alone. Greg, would you please step outside?"

The young man looked annoyed but left. Then Kurt leaned forward confidentially.

"I thought it best not to upset Greg about what I'm going to tell you," he said. "Greg's a nice enough fellow, but he has no head for business. His grandfather knew that. At one time Elias Woodson planned to leave the school to him but changed his mind."

The Hardys were astonished at the statement. This certainly complicated matters.

"When did Mr. Woodson make this decision?" Frank asked.

"Oh, I don't know exactly," Kurt answered. "But soon after I'd come to work here, he recognized my ability and decided to bequeath it to me."

Frank and Joe looked at each other. A feeling of distrust was building in their minds.

"I'm worried about two things," Kurt continued. "First, the will of Elias Woodson has not been found. This hampers my efforts. And second, a mysterious character who uses a yellow feather as an insigne constantly threatened old Mr. Woodson, and now me, with both bodily harm and the burning of the school. Recently he sent me notes claiming that the school rightfully belongs to him!"

"This makes a three-cornered puzzle," Frank thought. He kept silent, however, as did Joe, waiting for Kurt to continue.

"One more thing," Kurt said. "I have filed application to become administrator of the estate since there is practically nothing in it but the school."

"How do you know that, Mr. Kurt?" Frank asked.

"From Elias Woodson himself," the headmaster quickly replied.

Frank and Joe looked quizzically at each other. Greg Woodson would not be happy to hear of this development!

"You may call Greg in now," Kurt said. "Tell him whatever you think best."

Joe went to get Greg, who returned and said to Kurt, "I think I'd prefer to talk to the Hardys alone, too. Frank and Joe, will you come to my room?"

"That seems fair enough," Frank agreed.

He and Joe excused themselves and went upstairs with Woodson to the school's guest room. It was located in the center of the building among the students' dormitories. Greg closed the door and the three sat down.

"Greg," Frank began, "how long before your grandfather died did he mention willing you the school?"

"At Christmas time. He spent the day with me. Why?"

"Because two other people are claiming the place belongs to them," Frank replied.

"What!" Greg exclaimed. "Who are they?"

"Kurt himself and the Yellow Feather!"

Greg's face whitened, then as the color returned he almost shouted, "The nerve of them! Woodson Academy belongs to me!"

Frank explained what Kurt had told him and Joe, adding that it now was imperative that they find the will, and also locate the Yellow Feather.

"It's going to be mighty uncomfortable staying here under the circumstances," Greg remarked. "But Kurt can't drive me away."

"He won't be easy to get along with," Joe prophesied. "Is he popular with the students?"

"He's a strict disciplinarian, the boys tell me," Greg replied. "He has his favorites, and most of the students know it. He spends a lot of time playing around with various inventions, too."

"Inventions!" Joe exclaimed.

"Yes. I hear he's a whiz at spring propulsion."

Greg was about to go on when Frank silently rose to his feet and held a finger to his lips. He had heard a floorboard creak in the hall. With a bound he reached the door and yanked it open.

An indistinct figure fled down the hall. Frank dashed out, but as he did, he tripped over an invisible obstruction and crashed to the floor!

CHAPTER III

A Surly Student

RUSHING out of the room, Joe and Greg stumbled headlong over Frank, who lay diagonally across the passageway.

Joe jumped up immediately. "Greg, give Frank a hand," he cried. "I'll go after that snooper." With that he sprinted down the hall.

Greg picked himself up, then helped Frank, who had been momentarily stunned. "Wow!" He grinned. "You guys bounced on me as if I was an air mattress!"

"Sorry about that," Greg said. "But—"

At that moment Joe reappeared. "The fellow got away!" he reported bitterly. "Not a trace of him. You all right, Frank?"

"Sure. I wonder what I tripped on."

Joe dropped to his knees. Running his fingers along the floor near the wall, his hand struck a length of wire. Pulling it taut, he discovered that it was knotted to a hook in the baseboard.

Stepping to the far wall of the corridor, Joe stooped down. There was a similar hook half pulled out of the wooden border. Evidently the wire had been attached to it.

"The eavesdropper rigged this up to ensure his getaway," Joe reported.

"Boy, it really worked!" Frank agreed.

Greg spoke up. "Did you get a look at him?"

"No," Frank replied, "but just before I fell I noticed one thing. As he turned the corner I saw his belt—it was wide and studded with silver nailheads."

"That's a good clue," Joe observed. "We'll track down every silver-studded belt in the place!"

"There can't be more than twenty-five students staying here between semesters," Greg said. "It'll be lunchtime soon and we can look them over."

While waiting for the luncheon bell, Frank said he would like to familiarize himself with the layout of the school.

"I'll show you around," Greg offered.

Before starting the tour, he notified Mrs. Teevan, the cook, that the Hardys would be his luncheon guests. Then he asked them to follow him.

"The left wing of this building contains only bedrooms," he said. "To the right of the center sections are the offices, classrooms, labs, and dining hall."

One end of the second-floor corridor opened into a large attractive library and study hall with windows along the north and south walls.

As the group returned up the hallway, Greg paused before a locked door. "This was Grandfather's study. I lost the key, so I can't show it to you right now. I searched it, though, and found nothing."

The tour was interrupted by the bell in the tower pealing noontime.

Singly and in pairs, the students straggled into the dining hall under the watchful eyes of the Hardys and Greg.

"Oh, oh, here comes a guy with a silver-studded belt, and look who he is!" Joe exclaimed.

"Benny Tass!" Frank murmured.

To Greg, the name meant nothing. To the Hardys, however, Tass was a familiar Bayport visitor. A senior at the Academy, he spent a great deal of his free time in town with a group of older boys and fancied himself to be a big shot.

When Benny spotted the Hardys he flushed and muttered an indistinct greeting.

Frank spoke up. "Benny, that's a good-looking belt you're wearing."

"Do the studs go all the way around?" Joe asked, flipping up Tass's coat.

"Hey, cut that out!" Benny blustered.

Frank stepped in front of Tass, blocking him.

"We were interested in the belt," he said, "because it looks just like one worn by somebody who was listening outside a certain door."

Benny fidgeted uneasily. "What door?"

"The one to the guest room! I'm trying to locate the person who strung a wire across the hall and tripped me."

Tass tried to hide a smirk but was not successful.

"Would you mind telling us," Joe demanded, "what you've been doing for the past two hours?"

"It's none of your business!"

With that, Tass elbowed past the trio and moved into the dining hall. Greg and the Hardys selected a table near the door and were soon enjoying a delicious lunch. When they had finished, Greg asked what the Hardys would like to do next.

"Shadow Benny Tass," Joe spoke up. "I'm not satisfied that he wasn't the snooper."

"The job's yours," said Frank. "I want to keep tabs on Kurt and learn more about the campus."

To Joe's disappointment, Benny spent most of the afternoon alone in his room. The only time he left it was to go to Kurt's office. The bits of conversation Joe could hear concerned a request of the student to drop his chemistry course for the second semester.

Frank learned nothing of importance either, but did get the layout of the school buildings clear in his mind—the field house and gymnasium, the riding stables, even the watchman's shed.

Just before six o'clock the Hardys started for home. On the bumpy snow-covered road, Frank became aware of another car behind him. Evidently the driver was in a hurry, for he blasted his horn continuously.

"All right, take it easy," Frank murmured, pulling as far to the right as he dared. "Wait till I find a place wide enough for you to get by."

But the other driver was too impatient. Roaring up, he started to pass with barely an inch of clearance. A second later he sideswiped Frank and there came the sound of ripping metal. The other car skidded slightly, righted itself, and raced off.

The Hardy convertible, out of control for a moment, skidded along a few feet, then Frank brought it to a stop. He and Joe got out to examine the damage. Angrily the boys stared at the twisted, crushed left fender.

"The idiot!" Joe cried. "That driver might have killed us!"

"And did you see his passenger?" Frank exclaimed. "He sure looked like Henry Kurt!"

"Good night!"

"By the way," Frank continued, pulling with

all his strength to get the fender away from the wheel, "did you get that car's license number?"

"No," Joe replied. "I kept watching where we'd end up."

"Same with me," his brother said ruefully. "Maybe there's another clue. I'm going to find that guy and make him pay for the damage!"

"Look at this!" interrupted Joe, bending down in the glare of the headlights.

Clearly outlined in the hard-packed snow were the tracks of the speeding car. One of them indicated that the left rear snow tire had a deep cut in it.

"This is a good lead," Joe stated.

"You're right," Frank agreed. He pulled a pad and pencil from his pocket and made a sketch of the evidence.

The boys drove the rest of the way home without incident. Upon arriving, they found a telephone message from Chet stating that he wanted them to meet him at Biff Hooper's cabin up the river late the following morning.

"We can't let him down," Frank said.

Early the next day the boys took their car to a garage to be repaired. Then they set off to do several errands for their mother. They were walking briskly out of a hardware store when a familiar voice stopped them short.

"Frank and Joe! It seems like ages since we last saw you!"

Spinning around, the brothers faced two attractive girls.

Frank smiled at the one who had called to them. "Hello, Callie!"

"Hi, Iola!" Joe said, grinning.

Callie Shaw and Iola Morton, Chet's sister, were classmates of the Hardys at Bayport High. Iola, who had shoulder-length dark hair, a tilted nose, and twinkling eyes, dated Joe for school dances. Callie, blond and vivacious, always accompanied Frank.

"You boys look as if you were on the trail of international spies—or something equally as dangerous!" Callie teased.

"You're right about the danger," Joe replied, laughing. "As a matter of fact, we're headed for the river to take a ride on Chet's new propeller sled."

"Oh, that awful thing!" Iola exclaimed. "Better tell that brother of mine to be careful or you'll end up in the hospital."

"We have another reason for wanting all three of you to stay in one piece," Callie added with a smile at Frank. "You're invited to take us on a sleigh ride next week."

Frank winked at his brother. "Okay, girls. If we survive this afternoon's ride we'll go."

The boys said good-by and headed home. After a quick lunch they borrowed their father's car and rode to the Hooper cabin. Rangy

Biff, who had come with Chet, greeted them enthusiastically when they arrived.

"See what this character's done now," he said. "Chet's put snow runners on his propeller sled and wants to take us for a ride in the woods."

"Sure, it's all set," Chet told them as he revved up the motor. "Hop on!"

The sled worked to perfection. Traveling along an old trail that curved and wound among the trees, it moved over the rolling countryside in an effortless glide. Suddenly Joe gripped Frank's arm and pointed.

"Look! Those tire tracks ahead!"

Stretching out before them were the telltale marks of an automobile. Every few feet along the left track was the indication that one of the tires had a deep cut in it!

Joe signaled Chet to stop and they all got off the sled, while Frank told the story of the wild driver the evening before.

"The same track as that—" Frank was saying when Joe exclaimed:

"And there's the car, parked up ahead!"

"And look who's beside it," Biff cried in amazement. "Benny Tass—with a rifle in his hands!"

CHAPTER IV

Unwanted Detectives

"WHEW, I'm glad Benny isn't pointing that gun at us!" Chet muttered.

The boys' surprise at seeing him with a rifle was nothing compared to the look of amazement on the face of Benny Tass when he saw them hurrying toward him. Hastily he tried to conceal the weapon, sliding it through a rear window of the car.

"Well, Benny," Frank greeted him, "this is very interesting. Why are you carrying a gun?"

"What's that to you?" the bully snapped.

"It just happens that this property is posted against hunting!" Joe told him. "Look at all the signs around here."

"Leave me alone!" Benny cried. "This land belongs to the Academy. I got permission!"

The boys were startled. "From whom?" Frank asked sharply.

"Mr. Kurt!" Benny shot back. "He told me a couple of weeks ago I could hunt any time I felt like it. And he's temporary headmaster—so I guess his word's good enough!"

Lacking proof to refute Benny's claim, Joe tried a new tack. "This your car, Benny?"

"Yes, it is. So what?"

"Plenty. I think it's the one that hit our convertible last evening and almost knocked us into a ditch!" Frank retorted, his eyes blazing.

"You're crazy! It wasn't me!" Benny shouted, clenching his fists. "Besides, if it was at night, how could you identify the car?"

Joe pulled out the pad and compared his sketch with the imprint from the left rear tire of Benny's automobile.

"Your car has the same cut tire that the other one had!" he challenged.

Benny was purple with rage. "I wasn't even out last night," he screamed.

"Didn't you ever notice that cut in your tire?" Joe pressed the attack, pointing to a deep gouge.

"Sure, it's been there a couple of weeks," Benny blustered. "Maybe somebody else has a cut tire too. You guys make me sick. I'm getting out of here."

"Not so fast," Frank told him.

He looked carefully at both bumpers. It must have been one of them which had crumpled the convertible's fender. But there seemed to be no new scratches on either of them. Was Frank wrong in his assumption, or had Benny polished the chrome surface to eradicate the evidence?

As Frank paused, Benny jumped into his car and slammed the door. The motor roared, the wheels spun on the snowy ground, and the youth veered off among the trees.

"We may as well head back ourselves," Joe proposed.

As the propeller sled skimmed over the snow with its four passengers, Frank said, "Even if we couldn't prove it, I'm sure it was Benny's car that sideswiped us last night. If Kurt was with him, and Kurt really gave Benny permission to carry a gun, I'd say the two are buddies. Funny combination."

"And we'd better keep an eye on them," Joe added.

Back at the Hoopers' cabin, the quartet broke up. Chet and Biff headed for town. The Hardys drove toward Woodson Academy.

"There's Skinny Mason!" Joe called out as they went up the long drive to the school. "Let's stop and talk to him."

The boy, reporting that he had suffered no ill effects from his icy bath in the river, was so grateful to his rescuers that he embarrassed them with his thanks.

"That's all right, Skinny," Joe told him. "Maybe someday you can help us out."

"Perhaps you can give us some information right now," Frank suggested. "Do any of the students here at the Academy have hunting privileges?"

"Only one that I know of—Benny Tass. He's Mr. Kurt's pet," the boy replied matter-of-factly. "Everybody in school knows that. Mr. Kurt gave him a scholarship to come here so he could play basketball on our team."

"I thought Woodson only gave scholarships for good grades!" Frank exclaimed.

"I don't think anybody had one before Benny," Skinny said. "And the funny thing is that he is only about the third best player on the team."

Frank and Joe were puzzled. Why should Kurt have made such an outright exception to regular school policy?

It occurred to Frank that Skinny might become an ally in helping them solve the mystery of the Yellow Feather.

"Did you ever hear of a guy who calls himself the Yellow Feather?" he asked.

"No," Skinny replied. "What is he—a fighter?"

The Hardys laughed. "We don't know whether he is or not, but we'd like to find him. If you hear anything about him, let us know."

"I sure will," Skinny promised. "Anything else I can do for you?"

As Frank pondered, Joe remarked, "Skinny,

ever since Greg Woodson showed up here with a strange letter from his grandfather, this mystery about the Yellow Feather has become more of a puzzle."

Skinny Mason's eyes popped. "You wouldn't be talking about a letter that old Mr. Elias Woodson wrote to young Mr. Woodson, would you?" he asked.

"Why, yes. What do you know about—?"

Before Joe could finish, the boy broke in excitedly, "I've been wondering about that letter ever since I mailed it."

"You?" Joe exclaimed.

"Well, the day old Mr. Woodson died," Skinny related, "I walked past the library and I saw an envelope on the ground."

"Go on," Frank urged.

"So I picked it up. The envelope was all addressed and stamped and ready to mail. I could see that it was in old Mr. Woodson's writing— he had a funny little shaky handwriting. I meant to mail the letter right away, but I forgot."

"When did you mail it?" Frank asked.

Skinny paused to reflect.

"Oh, right after I found the envelope they told us we'd have three days off from classes because of the headmaster's death. I got halfway home before I noticed the letter was still in my pocket. Then I dropped it off at the post office."

"Greg did mention that the address looked

washed out," Joe remarked. "It must have been caused by lying in the snow. But I wonder how it got there."

"I think I can figure that part out," Frank said.

Before he could explain, Skinny said he must leave because he had an appointment with one of his teachers. The Hardys thanked him for his help and said they would see him again soon. After the boy had gone, Frank continued:

"Mr. Woodson must have been working on the cutout paper in the library and just finished addressing the envelope when he was interrupted by someone. Apparently he didn't want this person to see the letter, so he dropped it out the window, meaning to retrieve it as soon as he could."

Joe nodded. "Only he was so ill he never had a chance to get the letter and died shortly afterward."

"I wonder if Henry Kurt might have been the one who walked in on him," Frank mused. "Perhaps we can find out. Let's go!"

The Hardys headed for the headmaster's office. As Frank was about to rap on Kurt's door, he stopped suddenly. Somebody inside was talking excitedly.

"Those Hardys ought to be kept away from here!" shouted a rough, angry voice. It was Benny Tass's.

"They're a couple of snoopers, all right," Kurt agreed. "So is that smart aleck of a grandson."

"Well, you ought to get 'em all out of here," Benny told him. "They're going to make trouble."

Joe stared at Frank with a quizzical smile at the thought of Kurt and Benny worrying over their detective work. Should they try to talk to Kurt now or postpone the interview?

The boys' decision was made for them when they heard someone whisper, *"H-s-s-st!* Frank! Joe!"*

Skinny Mason had come up behind them, and was impatiently signaling them.

"Greg Woodson's awful sick," he said in a low voice. "He wants you right away. He—he thinks maybe he's been poisoned!"

Following Skinny, the Hardys rushed off to aid Greg. They found him lying on one of the twin beds in the guest room.

"It's my stomach!" he said weakly.

"Skinny, get the school nurse," Frank ordered.

As the boy hurried off, Greg said, "I feel better now. I got only a small amount of the poison, I guess."

"How?" Joe asked.

Greg pointed to a tray on his desk. It contained a small plate on which was an untouched sandwich and a saucer bearing a nearly full cup of coffee.

"You drank some of this?" Frank queried.

Greg nodded. "Then I saw what was under the cup—too late."

Frank, curious, reached over and raised the cup. Underneath, lying in the middle of the saucer, was a small yellow feather!

CHAPTER V

An Odd Bookmark

THE Hardys stared at the yellow feather and the poisoned cup of coffee.

"Greg, you're in real danger. This Yellow Feather guy means business." Frank paused, then asked, "Where did this tray come from?"

"Why, now that you ask me, I don't know. It was on the desk when I walked in."

"This is a school tray," Frank remarked, seeing the engraved Woodson monogram.

Joe was about to express an opinion when Skinny dashed in to say that the school nurse was on vacation.

"I'm feeling much better," Greg said. "We'll forget about nurses and doctors. Thanks, Skinny."

When the boy left, Joe said, "Before we do anything else, I think we ought to find out what's in this coffee. Can we get into the chem lab, Greg?"

"Sure. The instructor has a key. I'll get it."

"Better not tell him what's up," Frank advised.

"Okay. He knows I'm a chem major," Greg said, "so he'll probably think I'm working on an assignment."

He went for the key and led the Hardys upstairs to the laboratory. It did not take long to find out that the coffee, indeed, contained poison.

"But why is the Yellow Feather so determined to get you out of the way?" Frank wondered.

"Don't forget, this fiend has threatened Kurt, too," Joe reminded the others.

"It can't be just because of this school," Frank said. "Woodson couldn't be a big money-maker, no matter who was headmaster. I believe there's a lot more to this mystery than any of us knows."

Greg was thoughtful. "Do you suppose some treasure's hidden here?" he asked.

"It's anybody's guess," Frank replied. "But one thing I'm sure of. You shouldn't stay at the Academy. Your life's in danger."

"Why not go back to Myles and leave us here to take care of things?" Joe proposed.

"I was going today, anyway," Greg told them. "Classes start tomorrow."

The boys returned to his room and waited

while he packed his suitcase. Then the Hardys accompanied Greg to his car. With a promise to keep him posted, they waved until he was out of sight.

"Let's question Mrs. Teevan and see if we can find out anything," Frank proposed.

"Good idea," Joe replied.

The cook, a stout, elderly lady with white hair, was washing dishes when the boys entered the kitchen. They introduced themselves as friends of Greg.

"We just came to ask about a tray that was sent to the guest room," Frank said.

"Oh, that," Mrs. Teevan answered. "Well, there was a note on the counter that told me to send a sandwich and coffee to Mr. Greg's room," she explained. "It was here when I came in from my last checkup in the dining hall."

"Who left it?" Joe asked.

Mrs. Teevan shrugged. "It wasn't signed."

"Have you got the note?" Frank asked.

"No. I put it in the incinerator a few minutes ago. I didn't see any point in keeping it."

"The handwriting could have been a clue," Frank mused. "After you read the note, what did you do?"

"I prepared the tray and my helper—a young girl who comes in for part-time work—carried it to the guest room. She said nobody was there so she left it on the desk."

"Did you put a little yellow feather under the coffee cup?" Joe shot the question at her.

Mrs. Teevan looked so puzzled the boys knew that she was innocent, and explained about Greg's sudden illness and the discovery of the tiny yellow feather beneath the cup of poisoned coffee.

The woman was aghast. "Surely you don't think I would try to poison Mr. Greg!"

Mrs. Teevan sank into a chair. The Hardys hastily assured her that she was not suspect, but by now she was very upset.

"Yellow feather! Where did I hear that before?" she repeated over and over again. "Was it old Mr. Woodson who mentioned it? I wonder—"

Frank and Joe urged Mrs. Teevan to try to remember.

"I can't seem to," the woman replied finally. "Why don't you talk to my husband? He's custodian of the grounds. Right now he's at our cottage."

The boys said they would question Mr. Teevan at once. First, though, they spoke to the cook's helper. The girl denied any knowledge of what had happened to the coffee after she had put the tray on the desk.

Frank and Joe hurried to the caretaker's cottage.

"Hello, boys," he greeted them affably. "I don't believe I know you. But come in."

The Hardys told him who they were and followed him inside.

"I've been relaxing with a mystery story," Mr. Teevan remarked as he invited the boys to sit down. "I'll just mark this page so I'll know where I am. Then we—"

"Wait! I mean, pardon me!" Joe exclaimed. "May I see that marker, please?"

Mr. Teevan passed the book to him. Joe showed the marker to his brother.

It was a small yellow feather!

"What's wrong?" the old man asked as he watched their tense faces.

"This bookmark!" Frank burst out. "How do you happen to be using a yellow feather, Mr. Teevan?"

"Oh, that! Why, we had a pet canary," the caretaker explained. "The bird died over a year ago, and after I buried it I found one little feather near its cage. I kept it for sentimental reasons."

His explanation had such a ring of sincerity that the Hardys accepted it without question. They mentioned that Mrs. Teevan had suggested their coming to see him, and gravely described the series of incidents that had preceded the attempt to poison Greg Woodson.

As the implications of the case sank in, Mr. Teevan paled visibly. "But Martha and I wouldn't have anything to do with—" he protested. "Why, my wife and I have been here at the Academy for more than ten years."

"We're simply trying to track down every clue we can to the identity of the Yellow Feather," Frank told him quietly. "Can you help us at all?"

When the elderly man failed to speak, Joe prompted him. "Have you ever heard anything that might help us? Your wife seemed to remember some connection with a yellow feather and old Mr. Woodson. Does that sound familiar to you?"

He pressed his hand to his forehead. "I don't know," he muttered. "It does seem familiar, but— Let me think."

For several moments the elderly man remained motionless and silent. Then he raised his head.

"Yes, I remember now. It was about a month before Elias Woodson died. He came here to leave an order for me to get in town and happened to see my little feather bookmark lying on the table."

"Yes?" Joe asked tersely.

"Mr. Woodson picked up the feather and examined it, then gave me a very strange look," Mr. Teevan went on. "He mumbled something about a yellow feather getting people into trouble. I didn't understand what he meant."

"He never explained?" Frank prompted.

"No. He was getting pretty feeble. I thought it was just a case of his mind wandering, so I didn't press him for an explanation."

Frank was about to ask for more details when the door of the cottage opened and Mrs. Teevan walked into the room. Weakly she groped for a chair.

"Martha, what's wrong?" her husband cried, helping the tottering woman to a seat.

"I'm so upset about this yellow feather business that I feel sick," she wailed. "I couldn't stay in that kitchen another minute. The girl will have to get dinner alone tonight."

"I'm very sorry we disturbed you," Frank said apologetically. "Please forget the whole thing."

"Forget!" she sobbed. "To think I was almost implicated in nearly causing Mr. Greg's death!"

"But everything turned out all right," Joe assured her.

"Yes, thank goodness. But I'm going to be accused," Mrs. Teevan sobbed. "I fixed that coffee and it had poison in it!"

The Hardys' concern for her welfare mounted as they realized the woman was close to hysteria.

"We'd better call a doctor," Frank advised, and moved across the room to the telephone.

"I'll stay here until he arrives," Joe offered. "Frank, you go back to the Academy and see what else you can find out."

"All right. Meet me near the gym in an hour," Frank agreed.

He left the cottage and headed for the main building. H took a little-used trail and was deep in thought when he gave a sudden start. The young sleuth had heard the rustle of branches in a large cluster of rhododendron which he had just passed.

He turned quickly but was too late. His arms were pinned to his sides and he was dragged from the path, struggling helplessly.

Frank glimpsed two masked faces as a gag was shoved into his mouth!

CHAPTER VI

Framed!

ONE hour later Mrs. Teevan was resting comfortably under the doctor's care, so Joe strode up to the gymnasium to meet his brother. Seeing Skinny Mason, he called to him, "Have you seen Frank?"

"No. But there's a pickup hockey game on the pond. Maybe he went over there. I'll show you where it is."

"I doubt it," Joe thought. Where could his brother have gone? And what was he doing? Had he run into trouble?

"Well, I'll take a look on the pond anyway," Joe decided.

Skinny led him to a ravine in which a frozen pond afforded a fine ice rink. There was no sign of Frank.

"Say, Skinny, we'd better start searching,"

Joe said apprehensively. Worried that perhaps the Yellow Feather had caught up with Frank, he led the way back to the Teevans' cottage.

"Frank intended to go straight to the gymnasium from here," Joe told Skinny. "That would mean this way."

With his young assistant, Joe walked slowly along the flagstone path, trying to pick out his brother's footprints in the few patches of snow that were left. Suddenly Skinny stopped at a large planting of rhododendron.

"Hey, look at this!" he cried, pointing.

All around the front of the bushes were clusters of footprints.

"It seems there's been a real struggle here," Joe said. "And I'm sure Frank was involved in it."

"I'll check behind those bushes," Skinny offered.

"Wait! Let me go first," Joe ordered.

He had hardly pushed the branches aside and started down an incline when he uttered a cry and raced ahead. Half-hidden by more shrubs, a trussed figure lay twisting and squirming in a snowbank below.

"It's Frank!" he shouted.

Joe quickly removed the gag; then whipped out his pocketknife. Skinny, who had caught up to him, watched him cut through the bonds.

Frank was stiff from the cold. Joe helped him to his feet and he moved around to revive his circulation. Then he told how the two masked figures had caught him by surprise.

"Did you get a look at them?" Joe asked.

"No. They wore ski masks. But it wouldn't surprise me," he continued, "if one of them were Benny Tass!"

"What makes you think that?"

"One was exactly Benny's size and build. And he'd want to get square for our accusing him of running into our car."

"Right. And now, we'd better get you home," Joe insisted.

As the boys walked through the woods, Skinny spoke up for the first time.

"Gee, Frank, you might have frozen to death," he said. "Do you really think Benny's that bad?"

The Hardys realized that in their excitement they had taken Skinny into their confidence—perhaps unwisely. If he mentioned this to any of the other boys, it might endanger their work. Joe was just about to ask Skinny to guard their secret when the boy saved him the trouble.

"You don't want me to say anything about this, do you?" he asked. "But I'll watch Benny Tass if you like and let you know what I find out."

"Thanks," Joe said. "You could be a great help!" Skinny's chest swelled with pride. As they reached the campus, he announced that he was going to start shadowing Benny at once and left them.

"Before we go home, Joe," said Frank, "I think we ought to tell Kurt about the coffee incident. And we'll have to report it to the police."

"Okay. I'll do it. You get in the car and turn on the heater," Joe proposed.

He hurried off to the headmaster's office but the man was not there. After asking a student where Kurt's bedroom was, Joe went to it and knocked.

Kurt poked his head out. His manner was anything but cordial.

"May I come in?" Joe requested. "I have something very private to talk to you about."

"Private?" Kurt repeated. He looked more annoyed than curious. "Well, all right, come in. But I'm very busy. I can give you only a minute."

"It won't take that long to save your life," Joe retorted, annoyed by the man's attitude.

"What do you mean?" Kurt flared.

Briefly Joe told the story of the poisoned coffee, suggesting that the headmaster be wary of a similar incident. To the boy's amazement Kurt broke into a sardonic laugh.

"Well, if I ever heard of a ridiculous story, that's it!" he exclaimed.

Joe felt hot anger rising in him at the man's reaction.

"My story is straight," he said. "And I'm going to report the incident to Chief Collig of the Bayport police."

Instantly Kurt's attitude changed. He mumbled an apology. "I thought you were joking. Now, in regard to the police—let me handle it. I don't want the story spread all over the school. I'll call the chief and explain."

Joe gave him a cold stare. "Well, okay," he said and left. He hurried to the car, jumped in, and slammed the door. As Frank started the motor, he remarked:

"What's up? You look pretty upset."

After telling Frank of Kurt's cutting remark, Joe added, "I guess he doesn't think much of us as detectives."

"Don't let it bother you," Frank advised. "And, by the way, we'd better not mention my little adventure at home. No use worrying Mother."

Joe agreed, and added, "What do you say we go back to the Academy tonight when no one's expecting us and do some sleuthing?"

"Good thought."

After dinner Frank and Joe picked up their repaired convertible and set off. Joe parked the car on a side road near the school grounds, and from there they made their way on foot to the apparently deserted campus. Few lights were in the windows of the main building.

Suddenly Frank gripped Joe's arm. "See that

light over the dining room—isn't that Elias
Woodson's study?"

"Sure is. Somebody must have sneaked in.
I'm going to take a look!" Joe announced.
When the boys reached the bay window beneath the study, he added, "Give me a hand up,
will you?"

Frank bent over and Joe climbed to his
shoulders. From there he was able to haul himself onto the sloping roof below the study window. Cautiously he raised his eyes to the level of
the sill.

In the dim light Joe could see a man in a dark
overcoat and hat, his back to the window, busy
examining the drawers of a desk which stood
against the opposite wall. Evidently disgusted
at not finding what he wanted, the man slammed
them shut, one after another.

Then he turned. He was completely masked!
Joe's heart pounded with excitement. Was this
the Yellow Feather?

The boy watched for several seconds as the
masked figure began a thorough search of the
rest of the room.

"Maybe we can trap him in the study," Joe
thought and started to climb down.

But as he moved he lost his footing on the
sloping roof. Unfortunately the noise alerted
the masked man. As Joe grabbed the sill, he saw
the intruder make for the door and disappear.

With a warning cry to his brother, Joe swung himself to the ground. In a few whispered words he told what had happened.

Together the boys dashed to the main entrance of the building, hoping to catch the intruder. As they reached it Frank and Joe were halted by a sudden command.

"Stop where you are!"

The voice, coming from the doorway, had a ring of authority. The order was followed by the beam of strong flashlight which caught them squarely. Henry Kurt, bareheaded, stepped toward the Hardys, scowling.

"Oh, it's you two again!" he exclaimed, clicking off his light. "I thought you were students breaking rules. What are you doing, anyway?"

"Mr. Kurt!" Joe cried. "I just saw a masked man in Mr. Woodson's study. Help us catch him!"

The headmaster stared at them in disbelief. "Nonsense! How could you see anyone in an upstairs room with no light in it? That room is locked, anyway."

"I know what I saw," Joe insisted. "We must—"

As if he were placating small children, Kurt stepped aside and let the boys in. "Go ahead and look."

He followed them up the stairs. The study

The man was completely masked

door was locked and no crack of light showed beneath it.

"I hope this satisfies you," Kurt remarked with exaggerated politeness. "I'm sorry I have no key or I'd let you in. And now, with this farce behind us, I have something to say to you. You make up such fantastic stories about other people breaking into private property. But what about yourselves?"

"What do you mean?" Frank asked. "We have permission to work on the mystery of the Yellow Feather. *Your* permission. We haven't broken into any place."

"Then what were you doing in my private office?" Kurt stormed.

Joe was indignant. "We weren't there!"

"Come with me!" Kurt commanded. "I have proof that you not only were there, but broke in!"

Thunderstruck at the headmaster's charge, the Hardys followed him downstairs.

"What in the world is he up to now?" Joe whispered to his brother.

"I have no idea what he's talking about. But I guess we'll find out."

Kurt reached the office and pointed to the door. "First of all," he said, "the lock has been jimmied. Quite obvious, isn't it?" His tone was sarcastic.

The boys inspected the spring lock of the

door and saw that the mechanism, indeed, had been forced.

"What makes you think *we* did it?" Frank asked angrily.

"I came in here tonight to go over some papers," Kurt said icily, "and found this!"

He walked ahead inside and stopped before the table. On it was a man's hand-knitted scarf. Woven into it were the initials F. H.!

"My scarf!" Frank cried.

"Just as I thought," Kurt said triumphantly. "Now suppose you explain what it is doing in my private office."

Embarrassed, Frank fingered the scarf, a Christmas gift from Callie Shaw. Quickly he thought back over the day's events. Then suddenly he snapped his fingers.

"Now I know!" he exclaimed, looking Kurt straight in the eyes. "This scarf was stolen from me this afternoon during a scuffle."

"Which means," Joe added, "that someone tried to frame my brother by planting it here."

Kurt glanced incredulously from one boy to the other, waiting to hear more.

"And if you want to know whom I suspect," Frank went on, "it's Benny Tass."

The headmaster started in surprise. Then quickly regaining his composure, he said. "Ridiculous! Tass is one of our finest boys."

Frank and Joe made no comment.

"Besides," Kurt went on, looking at Frank, "why would Tass want to frame you?"

"That's something we'd like to find out," Frank replied. "He seems to have gone out of his way to make things uncomfortable for us."

He explained about the near accident in the car the previous night, watching the man carefully to see if he would show any sign that he had been with Benny. But Kurt's face remained expressionless.

Then Frank gave details of the attack on him that morning.

"Oh, bosh!" Kurt exploded. "In no case are you sure that Tass was a guilty party. And I'm convinced he wasn't. As far as hunting is concerned, I did give him permission, because he's older and more responsible than the other boys here."

"Then have you any idea who planted my scarf in your office?" Frank asked.

"Well, since you insist that you didn't force your way in here, there's only one answer. I believe it might have been the Yellow Feather. He attacked you and left the scarf to throw suspicion away from himself."

Kurt paused, then added, "And if he's going to prowl around here at night, it might be smart to have you boys on hand to track him down."

"I agree," Frank replied. "How about our starting tonight?"

"Very good. Take the guest room Greg vacated."

The boys thanked Kurt and turned to leave. Nearing the door they exchanged knowing glances. Not fully trusting the man, Joe left the door open a crack in case he should want to go back and check up on Kurt's movements.

The boys did not mention their thoughts aloud. But when they reached a pay telephone booth on one side of the corridor Frank paused and said in a loud voice:

"Joe, we'd better call Mother and tell her we're staying overnight."

While Frank dialed the Hardys' number, Joe stood outside, mulling over Kurt's sudden proposal.

"I wonder if he's laying some sort of trap for us?" Joe asked himself.

Walking back to the office, he could hear the headmaster moving noisily about inside. The door was still slightly ajar, affording him a view of the room without being seen himself.

Kurt stood in front of a filing cabinet. He drew out a bunch of small keys and inserted one into the lock at the top. Then he pulled the bottom drawer open and took out a folded piece of white paper.

After giving it a quick glance, the headmaster smiled, then put the paper in an inside pocket of his jacket and pushed the drawer shut.

As he walked toward the door, Joe dashed back to the telephone booth.

Frank had just hung up and was stepping from the booth when Kurt walked down the corridor and spied the boys.

"Hello! Not in your room yet?" he asked, evidently annoyed.

"We called home to report where we are," Frank replied.

This seemed to satisfy Kurt. He said good night and walked off.

"Well, what do you make of him?" Frank whispered as they climbed the stairs.

"Either Kurt's on the level or he's the biggest fraud alive," Joe replied.

When they reached the guest room, Joe told his brother of Kurt's actions in the office.

"What do you think was on that paper?"

"I'll bet it has something to do with the Woodson estate," Frank replied. "Kurt wouldn't be so sure he can get this school if he didn't have some kind of proof. For some reason he doesn't want to produce it yet, though."

"It would be a big help if we could get a look at that paper," Joe remarked as he lay down on one of the twin beds.

"Fat chance we have of checking Kurt's

pocket," Frank replied as he pushed up the window and peered outdoors. "Wow, it's sure cold tonight. Well, I guess we're safe from attack here." He laughed. "No roofs or trellises for anyone to climb."

Joe nodded. "Might as well turn in for the night." He snapped the lock on the door, switched off the light, and soon was sound asleep.

Frank had no idea how long he and Joe had been deep in slumber when he was suddenly awakened by a thud against the wall of the building. Springing out of bed, he rushed to the window and glanced out.

"Joe!" he whispered. "Come look!"

Directly beneath the sill was the top of a ladder! It trembled slightly under the weight of a shadowy figure climbing upward.

CHAPTER VII

A Thwarted Intruder

By this time Joe was awake. Seeing his brother at the window, he rushed over to him and looked out into the darkness. Silently the intruder on the ladder continued rung by rung toward the bedroom. It was impossible from this height to identify him.

"Let's wait till he steps in before we jump him," Frank whispered.

Both boys tensed, shivering a little as the cold wind blew against them. They pressed close to the wall at each side of the window.

Suddenly the ladder gave a twist and began to slide to one side. It scraped against the brick exterior, pulling ivy vines loose in its descent. It hit the snow with a muffled thump, and the would-be intruder was flung off into a pile of snow. He struggled to his feet, then dashed away into the night.

"What luck!" Frank exclaimed. "We almost had him!"

"Do you think that was the Yellow Feather trying to get us?" Joe asked excitedly.

Frank was already reaching for his trousers. "Come on, Joe. Let's go get that second-story man."

The boys flung on their clothes and tiptoed hurriedly downstairs. They met no one. Finding the spot where the man had fallen, the boys followed his trail of footprints for a hundred yards. But here they were lost in a maze of crisscross prints which students had made.

Returning to the ladder, Frank flashed his light about, hunting for clues in the snow beneath their window.

"Holy crow!" he exclaimed. "Two sets of footprints!"

"So the guy had an accomplice!" Joe remarked.

"But if that were the case," Frank said reflectively, "why did he let the ladder fall?"

"Beats me," Joe answered. "They sure were a couple of bunglers. Maybe two students playing a joke."

"I doubt that," his brother replied.

The rest of the night passed quietly. In the morning Frank sat on the edge of his bed, yawned, and stretched. Joe was already half-dressed.

"Toss me my pants, will you?" his brother requested as he looked for his shoes and socks.

"Where are they?"

"Right over there on the chair next to— Hey!" Frank leaped to his feet. "They're gone!"

A quick look around confirmed the fact that his slacks had been taken from the room.

Joe walked to the door and yanked it open. Someone had unlocked the door during the night!

"Jumpin' catfish!" he shouted. "Whoever stole your pants could have murdered us in our beds!"

"Could be that the prowler and the pants burglar weren't the same person," Frank commented. "But how am I going to get out of here without trousers?"

"Maybe we can borrow a pair." Joe chuckled. "I'll see what I can find out."

He had just stepped from the room when the noise of running feet and roars of laughter sounded through the corridor. Three young boys dashed wildly past. Joe recognized one of them.

"Skinny Mason!" he called. "What's all the hurry?"

"Somebody's pants are hanging from the bell tower!" The youngster giggled. "And they say Mr. Kurt is about to blow his top."

Joe followed Skinny down the stairs and outside. High above the school, on the very top of the tower, Frank's slacks were fluttering in the breeze!

Suddenly a voice hissed in Joe's ear, "You're a detective. How do you account for this?"

Joe wheeled around to face the headmaster. "I can't account for how the pants got up there," the chagrined Joe was forced to admit, "but I can tell you whose they are. They're my brother's!"

Kurt looked at Joe in disgust. Then he turned to one of the students standing nearby.

"I want every boy out here within five minutes," he ordered. "Pass the word."

It did not take long to round up the students. But when Kurt demanded that the culprit step forward, there was nothing but a general shuffling of feet.

"I'll get to the bottom of this!" Kurt thundered.

After telling them that such behavior reflected on the dignity of the school, he quizzed the students on what they knew about the tower itself.

"The stairs were condemned and torn down long ago," he stated. "Do any of you know another way the prankster could have reached the top?"

There was an uneasy silence until Benny Tass

spoke up. "Maybe someone climbed out from one of those attic windows onto the catwalk around the tower and just threw the pants to the top," he suggested. "But I don't know anything about it."

Joe went to get the ladder under the guest-room window. Kurt stormed for a few more minutes as to how the school ladder had gotten there. No one answered, and Joe asked Skinny to bring him a fish pole.

Then Joe propped the ladder against the wall, and holding the pole, climbed to the catwalk of the tower. A few flicks of his wrist and he cast the fishhook into Frank's pants. Amid cheers from the onlookers he hauled them down.

"Whose are they?" several boys asked.

Joe escaped without answering. When he brought them to Frank, his brother stared in astonishment. A rueful grin that spread over his face as Joe told the story lasted only a moment, then he began to speculate on who had taken the pants.

"Are you sure you locked our door the second time?" Joe asked him.

Frank thought a moment. "No, I'm not sure. Dumb of me. I deserve what happened."

"I'm glad it wasn't any worse," Joe remarked. "Well, let's get some breakfast and then start our sleuthing."

Several students had already assembled in

the dining hall. As Frank and Joe entered, Kurt met them, anger on his face.

"There's no breakfast," he announced. "The cook and her helper didn't show up this morning."

"Mrs. Teevan probably is still ill," Frank reminded him. "The doctor may have told her to stay in bed today."

"Doctor!" Kurt exclaimed. "I didn't know anything about that. What's the matter with her?"

Frank briefly explained the circumstances that led to the physician's visit. Kurt expressed no sympathy but burst out:

"That leaves us in a fine mess. And that assistant quit—just when we need her. I found her note of resignation on the kitchen counter top."

"Looks as if we'll have to get our own breakfast," Frank remarked.

"The Yellow Feather is behind all this!" Kurt said. "I'm sure of it. He's the one who left the note ordering that tray for Greg Woodson."

Suddenly the headmaster snapped his fingers. "Why didn't I think of it before!" he exclaimed.

Leaning over, he whispered confidentially, "The Yellow Feather must be nearby to make such frequent visits. I'll bet I know where his hideout is!"

"Where?" the Hardys chorused.

"The school has a camping hut along the

river," Kurt replied. "We'll find that scoundrel!"

"It might be a good idea to look," Frank agreed.

He and Joe walked into the kitchen with the intention of getting something to eat when Skinny, who had been looking everywhere for them, came to tell them that Chet was at the front door.

"Chet! Up this early!" Joe exclaimed. "Something important must have happened!"

The two boys hurried to the main entrance and looked questioningly at their friend. Quickly he explained that Mrs. Hardy had telephoned him to deliver a message to them.

"She said your dad was in touch with her and wanted you fellows warned that you're in danger out here!" Chet whispered.

How well they knew that! the Hardys thought. But how had their father learned this?

Quickly they brought their friend up to date on what had happened and Chet whistled softly.

"Say," Joe asked him, "how would you like to hang around and do some cooking? You might pick up some clues for us."

Chet beamed. "Direct me to the food supply."

Joe led the way and introduced him to the headmaster.

"I've found a cook!" he announced triumphantly.

"And not a bad one either!" Chet boasted. "I came up here on my sled to see what the Hardys were doing, and it looks as if I'll come in handy until your regular cook gets back to work, Mr. Kurt."

Frank explained Chet's fondness for food and remarked that he had developed a flair for the culinary art. Kurt readily agreed to the plan.

As a chef, Chet proved his ability to organize an efficient staff. Strutting about in an apron, he divided up the work so quickly between several boys that an excellent breakfast was prepared in short order.

During the meal Joe discussed Kurt's proposal with his brother and added, "It doesn't make sense that a criminal would be hiding in a hut which might be used by students at any time."

"The Yellow Feather probably knows that most of the boys are away," Frank pointed out.

"Oh, it's possible, all right," his brother agreed. "But I'm not putting much stock in Kurt's idea."

He contemplated another angle. "Maybe Kurt is trying to get us away from the school for some reason."

Frank shrugged. "Suppose I stay here while you and Kurt go to the hut."

Joe agreed. Frank told Kurt he wanted to help Chet get the kitchen setup organized and he would not make the trip to the hut. The headmaster looked displeased but said that he and Joe would proceed, anyway.

"We'd better go on skis," Kurt suggested, and arranged for Joe to borrow the equipment.

Gliding along through the woods, they soon reached a trail which Joe recognized as the one on which the boys had spotted Benny Tass with his car. As he was beginning to wonder if this were a favorite haunt of the unpleasant boy, Tass suddenly appeared at the side of the trail, leaning on ski poles.

"Hello, Mr. Kurt. Hi, Joe!" Benny greeted them. "What's up?" It was the friendliest he had ever been to the Hardy boy.

"Oh, we're just going to the camp-out hut," Kurt returned. "Want to come along?"

"Sure."

Joe noticed a sly smile creep over Benny's face as he joined them. Also, Kurt seemed a bit too pleased by the addition of the new arrival.

Mr. Hardy's warning flashed into Joe's mind. Had Kurt and Tass planned this? Was he walking into danger?

CHAPTER VIII

Snowbound

"I'm going to watch these two like a hawk!" Joe resolved silently.

But as they glided forward through the woods his anxiety lessened, for both Kurt and Tass seemed very friendly. To Joe's amazement the headmaster told Benny of the Yellow Feather mystery and the mysterious happenings in connection with it.

"Sure is spooky business," Benny said with a quaver. "I hope we don't find the Yellow Feather in the hut. He sounds like a guy to stay away from."

"It's my guess he's not there," Joe spoke up and to himself added, "Kurt wouldn't dare let a student run the risk of meeting such a dangerous person."

As the three moved on, the sun was blotted out. A biting wind cut their faces.

"More snow coming," Joe remarked. "We'd better make this trip snappy."

They came to a wooded hill and herringboned to the summit. Then swiftly the skiers slalomed to the bottom.

"Be quiet, boys," Kurt warned them. "We're getting close now, Joe. There's the hut up ahead."

Several hundred yards away Joe could see a solidly built little stone house which looked well cared for. Kurt explained that he and Mr. Teevan came out once in a while to make sure things were in order. Neither of them, however, had been here recently. As they neared the building, conversation ceased until Kurt burst out:

"Just as I thought! Someone's been living here!"

The boys noticed that the snow around the cabin had been trampled down in several directions.

"Look at that stack of logs by the door," Benny pointed out. "It wasn't there the last time I was out."

"You're right," Kurt agreed. "Let's surround the place. I'll move in from this side. You two circle and close in from the front and back."

At Kurt's signal they all advanced.

At the front door Kurt pounded and called. There was no reply.

Joe watched tensely in case the Yellow Feather should jump out a window. But there was not a sign of him.

The boys hurried to the door and followed Kurt inside. The hut was vacant. A quick scanning of the interior showed everything to be in order—the table clear, the sink clean.

Kurt sniffed the air several times and headed for the fireplace. With a poker he jabbed at the ashes. Little spots of red came to life.

"I thought so," he proclaimed. "Someone has been here!"

Joe did not share the man's excitement. "How about Mr. Teevan?" he asked.

Kurt gave a slight start, then said, "Impossible." He was standing before the fireplace, his eyes riveted to the mantel above. Bright against the gray stone lay a tiny yellow feather!

"I knew it!" Kurt gloated. "The Yellow Feather has been living here!"

Examining the feather, Joe realized it was similar to the one that had been left under Greg's coffee cup and the same kind which Mr. Teevan used as a bookmark.

"Didn't I tell you?" Kurt said excitedly. "That crook is living in this cabin, and disappearing whenever he thinks someone might show up."

"It sure does look like it," Benny agreed.

Joe was not paying attention. He was thinking about Mr. Teevan. This was the second time the caretaker had come under suspicion. Was he the Yellow Feather, or was someone trying to frame him?

Joe looked for other signs of occupancy, or a clue to who the intruder might have been. He found nothing.

"Well, I really ought to get back to school," Kurt remarked a few minutes later. "I have a lot of work to do before the rest of the boys return from vacation. But why don't you two stay here and see if you can't catch this Yellow Feather?"

"Sounds like a swell idea," Benny was quick to agree—a little too quick, Joe thought.

The idea of being left in the hut with Benny did not appeal to Joe. Furthermore, he wanted to keep track of Kurt.

"I think we'd better go back to school together," he said. "I can't see much sense in splitting our forces, and anyway, it's going to snow."

"You're not afraid to stay here, are you?" Kurt asked sarcastically.

Benny sneered, "I thought you and your brother were such brave detectives that lying in wait at a lonely hut wouldn't scare you at all."

Joe refused to be nettled.

"Our experience in detective work," he said calmly, "is exactly what makes me think it would be wise to look elsewhere for the Yellow Feather."

Kurt flushed at this observation but made no comment. They put on their skis in silence and set off. The raw wind howled through the bare trees and tore at the three figures. Before they had gone half a mile the sky grew dark and a driving snowstorm descended upon them.

"We're going to have trouble getting through this," Kurt remarked nervously as the snow matted in his beard. "I can't see ten feet ahead."

Before they had traveled a hundred yards farther, a heavy branch, weighted by snow and lashed by the wind, cracked and toppled down. It landed between Joe and Benny, who jumped several feet to avoid it.

"Maybe we should go back to the hut and wait this out!" Benny said worriedly.

Traveling on skis became impossible and they finally took them off. The snow was not only deep but coming down so thick that the group could see only a few feet ahead of them. Again a huge limb crashed down.

"Hey, I don't want to be conked!" Benny exclaimed. "And we're off the trail!"

At last the headmaster agreed that they had better return to the hut before their foot and ski prints were entirely covered by snow.

By the time they reached the stone building, they were exhausted. After propping their skis beside the door they carried in some of the stacked wood and soon had a comfortable blaze in the fireplace.

"This is most unfortunate, most unfortunate!" Kurt kept murmuring as he strode back and forth like a caged lion.

The snow seemed to be coming down even harder and continued to fall steadily after evening descended.

"I guess we'll have to spend the night here," Kurt said. "But at least we're safe from the Yellow Feather. He can't get back here."

They found several cans of food and sat gloomily around the fire to eat beans and corned-beef hash.

"We may as well go to bed right away," Benny suggested when they finished. "Then we can wake up early and get back to school. Let's bar those windows, and the door, too."

Joe helped secure the hut, then sat cross-legged in front of the fire.

"I think I'll sit up and keep this blaze going," he said, "while you sleep."

Reluctant at first, the other two agreed and settled themselves in the hut's bunks. Joe gazed thoughtfully into the leaping firelight. He tried to sift the events that seemed to tie in with the appearance of yellow canary feathers and the disappearance of old Elias Woodson's strange cutout message to Greg.

After some time Joe noticed that the fire was getting low. All the wood had been used up.

"I'll get an armload from the stack outside," he murmured to himself, and quietly opened the door.

Stepping out, he found that the storm finally had abated. Snow had covered the pile of logs, and it took Joe a few minutes to brush several inches of the white fluff away before he could begin to gather up a load.

Stooping over, the boy heard a muffled footstep behind him. As he straightened up, a blunt object connected with the back of his head.

Joe pitched forward and blacked out.

CHAPTER IX

Cat-and-Mouse Sleuthing

IN the library of Woodson Academy, Frank and Chet were poring over a pile of books. It was late afternoon and snow was pelting against the windows.

"This place would be too obvious for old Mr. Woodson to hide anything," Chet complained. "He'd never take a chance of some student stumbling upon it."

"I'm not so sure," Frank answered. "Sometimes the obvious is the most difficult to see."

Their examination of the school library was the final stop on a tour that produced nothing in the way of clues to the mystery.

"I thought your idea of a secret room, or passage, was better," Chet said regretfully. "I've always wanted to find a hidden treasure!"

Frank chuckled and agreed that he too had

been disappointed by their failure to find a cache. Taking advantage of Kurt's absence they had spent several hours tapping the inner walls of the building but without success.

Finally Frank, recalling Skinny's tale of finding Elias Woodson's letter to Greg below the library windows, had steered their course to that room. Having uncovered nothing, they were now about to give up for the day.

"Hm! Here's a row of yearbooks," Chet commented as they walked toward the door. "I'll bet they're full of funny old-time pictures."

As he pulled out a volume to look at it, Frank scanned the row.

"A lot of them are missing," he remarked. "Let's see—Dad's class is one of them." He wondered if the books had been borrowed by someone or whether the collection was simply incomplete.

"Let's call it quits," Chet said. "I'm getting hungry. Time to go back to my duties in the kitchen."

Frank agreed but said to count him out on helping. With Kurt's continued absence he wanted to do some more sleuthing.

"I just thought of something," he said.

"What?" Chet asked.

"I found a key in the guest-room closet on the floor under a pair of sneakers. They might be Greg's and he might have lost the key there."

"You think it'll open something here at school?" Chet questioned.

Frank nodded. "Maybe old Mr. Woodson's study."

As Chet started down to the kitchen, Frank went for the key and tried it in the study lock. The bolt moved and the door opened!

Frank locked himself in and got to work. It was an interesting room with heavy, carved furniture and paneled walls. For half an hour Frank tapped and searched. At last he came to the same conclusion Greg Woodson had: The deceased man's secret was not to be found here.

He returned to the guest room and hid the key in a dresser drawer under the paper lining. Then he went to the kitchen. Chet was busy at the stove, with several students running errands for him between the refrigerator, the sink, and the dining room. Among them was Skinny, who rushed over to Frank.

"Say, what do you suppose happened to Joe and Mr. Kurt and Benny Tass? They're all missing!"

Frank said he thought they must have been caught in the storm and had taken shelter.

"Maybe the camp hut," Skinny remarked.

Frank did not tell the boy why Joe and Kurt had gone there and wondered if Benny had joined them. As time went on and the storm abated a little Frank confessed to Chet that he was fearful that the Yellow Feather might have captured Joe and Mr. Kurt.

"Joe could have gone home," Chet suggested. "Why don't you phone and find out?"

"I'll do it," Frank said and hurried to the telephone booth.

Aunt Gertrude answered, and in reply to his query, she said Joe had not been there. She reported, however, that Fenton Hardy had been home for an hour but had gone out again, not telling his destination. He had requested that if his sons called to tell them the FBI had no record of anyone with the name of Yellow Feather.

"Your father also said to tell you," Miss Hardy went on, "that he thinks the paper Mr. Kurt left with him may be a fake. He doesn't trust Kurt and wants you to try hard to find the one Greg Woodson lost."

After Frank had completed the telephone call, he stood lost in thought a few minutes. Although Kurt had said that the cutout paper had been given to him by Elias Woodson, maybe he had found Greg's paper on the river and had made a copy of it. Had he slipped up on some detail which was apparent to Mr. Hardy?

"That paper Kurt took from the file cabinet and put in his pocket might have been the original!" Frank thought excitedly. "Fat chance I'd have of finding out, though!"

Suddenly another idea came to him. On a hunch he put in a call to Myles College. A fellow student in Greg's dormitory obligingly summoned the senior. Greg instantly asked if the Hardys had uncovered any new clues.

"Well, sort of," Frank answered. "Dad thinks the cutout paper Kurt left with him could be a phony. I may know where yours is, but I can't get it. Greg, do you think you could possibly remember those series of cutouts well enough to make a duplicate?"

"You mean to get all those little holes in exactly the same arrangement? I don't know. It'll be tough, but I'll try, Frank, if you really think it's important."

"I sure do."

Frank found Chet and they talked about the case, interspersing their conversation with remarks about Joe's long absence. Their worry increased with the passing hours, but when bedtime arrived, Chet tried to reassure Frank.

"Probably Joe is on the trail of that crook," he said. "Just wait and see."

The two boys retired to the school guest room. Chet took Joe's empty bed and slept soundly. But Frank tossed and turned a good part of the night because of his concern over his brother. Next morning his worry became intensified when Kurt, with Benny Tass behind him, strode into the dining hall.

"Good morning," they both said heartily.

"Where's my brother?" Frank asked.

Kurt looked surprised. "Isn't Joe here?"

After explaining that they had stayed at the hut overnight because of the storm, Kurt went on to say that he and Benny had been awakened early that morning by cold air blowing in through the open door of the cabin.

"I assumed that Joe had made a head start to the school. His skis were gone," the headmaster reported.

Frank leaped up from his half-finished breakfast. "I'm going out to find him!" he exclaimed. "Something has happened to Joe!"

"We'll organize a search party," Kurt proclaimed.

But Frank and Chet did not wait to hear more. Rushing from the dining hall, they almost bumped into Skinny Mason.

"Say, you know how to get out to that camp hut," Frank cried as he halted the boy. "Get your coat and lead the way, will you?"

Chet and Frank borrowed skis and poles, and before Kurt had even begun to gather an official search party, they were off through the woods with Skinny Mason. Fortunately, Skinny had a keen sense of direction and guided them easily to the hut. Winded and excited, they quickly determined that Joe had not returned to the shelter since the departure of Kurt and Benny.

"Where'd he go?" Skinny asked, wide-eyed.

"Say, look at this!" Chet called from near the woodpile. "There must have been some kind of commotion here."

Frank's sharp eyes surveyed the scene. The newly fallen snow of the blizzard was stomped down all around the stack of firewood.

"Something was dragged away through the woods!" he exclaimed, pointing to a trail of deep footprints in the snow. "Come on! Chet, Skinny, hurry!"

With ski poles working furiously, the boys made their way through the clearing into the woods again, and out onto the bank of the frozen Willow River.

"Looks as if the tracks lead to that old boathouse over there," Chet puffed as he followed Frank across the snow toward a rickety, unpainted shack near the river's edge.

One narrow door, half off its hinges, marked the end of the trail. Kicking off his skis, Frank yanked the door open and strode inside. The other boys waited tensely. In the dim light he saw a figure face downward, lying motionless in one corner. Frank turned the bound and gagged person over.

Joe!

With quaking heart Frank felt his brother's pulse. He was alive!

"Chet, help me bring him to!" Frank cried.

"Help me bring him to!" Frank cried

He removed the gag and with a pocketknife cut the bonds that had held his brother for so many hours. Then he and Chet gave him first aid. Finally Joe was restored to consciousness. He smiled feebly but could not speak.

"You must be half-frozen," Chet groaned in sympathy.

He and Frank carried Joe to the cabin. Skinny ran on ahead and by the time they arrived he had kindled a blaze in the fireplace.

After drinking some hot broth which Chet had prepared, Joe recovered from his ordeal sufficiently to tell the others of the attack upon him.

"You don't think Mr. Kurt or Benny did it?" Skinny asked, aghast.

Frank and Joe exchanged glances but did not reply.

"It must have been the Yellow Feather," Chet decided.

"I don't know," Joe replied glumly. "I wish I'd seen him, but I didn't."

An hour later he declared that he was able to start back to the school.

"My skis ought to be somewhere outside," he said.

"Unless they were stolen," Chet remarked.

Skinny, taking a quick turn around the cabin, found the skis half-buried in the snow and soon the four boys were ready to start back. Plodding along with Frank and Chet on either side of him, Joe proceeded steadily.

As they approached the school, Frank caught a glimpse of the headmaster moving about in his office.

While Chet and Skinny continued across the campus, the Hardys entered the building. As they walked in on Kurt, he whirled to face his unexpected visitors. His face was a mirror of astonishment.

"You're back, Joe!" he exclaimed in a flustered tone. After a pause he added, "Fine! Fine! I was rather worried. The way you went off, I didn't know— Joe, I'm really glad to see that you're safe. I sent out a search party but they couldn't find you. What happened?"

As the young detectives explained, they watched Kurt's face but all it showed was incredulity.

"Terrible, terrible!" Kurt exclaimed. "The Yellow Feather really means business. This case is getting completely out of hand. I think you had better let your father take over."

"Not a chance!" Joe burst out. "We're solving this mystery for Greg Woodson! And what's more we want a key to this building."

"Have it your way, then," Kurt said, and reluctantly handed him an extra key. "But I'll not be held responsible for the outcome."

Leaving the office, the Hardys ran into Benny Tass who also appeared surprised to see Joe. He gave him a half-hearted welcome and added:

"You guys must be crazy to play around with that Yellow Feather. He may be a killer!"

"We'll take that chance," Frank said as he and Joe moved off.

The Hardys went to the dining room. They enjoyed Chet's good lunch and Frank told Joe about finding the key to the study. They had just finished eating when Greg Woodson came in. He explained that he had been given several days' leave from college.

"I've been appointed administrator of my grandfather's estate!" he announced proudly. "The court handed down the decision yesterday."

"Has Kurt heard this yet?" Frank asked, immensely pleased at the news.

"I don't know, but here he comes."

When the headmaster heard Greg's news, he broke into a torrent of complaints against the legal decision about which he had just been informed by telephone.

"You—you—" He pointed a menacing finger at Greg. "You're young, inexperienced! What do you know about business? Nothing!"

Greg was furious. "Mr. Kurt," he said, his eyes blazing, "if you weren't older and headmaster here, I'd punch you right in the nose!"

The angry, raised voices instantly drew all the students from the tables. They gathered in a circle around the two men, expecting a fight.

"Greg can lick him!" one whispered.

The remark seemed to bring Kurt to his senses. He ordered the boys back to their tables, then turned on his heel and left.

After telling of the attack on Joe, the Hardys informed Greg of their growing suspicion against Kurt and that he might even be trying to harm them.

"We haven't been able to figure out why," Frank admitted, "but we're going to keep a closer watch on him from now on."

"And on Benny Tass," Joe added.

Frank asked Greg if he had made a copy of the cutout letter.

"Not yet, but I'll do it right now," he replied.

Seated in the guest room with them, he painstakingly penciled a series of small rectangles on a sheet of stationery, then cut them out.

"This is about as close as I can make it from memory," he said hopefully and held it up.

The Hardys studied the sheet carefully for several minutes, then Frank said, "I believe that your grandfather designed the sheet to cover a certain page in a book. The cutout places will reveal a message."

Greg was impressed. "But what book?" he queried.

"Well, if your grandfather was working on it in the school library the night before his death," Joe declared, "the book is probably there."

'Let's start a search," Greg proposed.

"How about the size of the book page?" Frank asked. "Is this sheet about the same size as the one you lost?"

Greg examined it for a few moments. "I'd say this might be a trifle larger than the other sheet."

Frank recommended that they wait until evening when no students would be in the library. Around eight o'clock, with Chet on guard at the door, Greg and the Hardys went to work. Greg chose the size volumes on which they would start, and a systematic search began.

They fitted the cutout sheet over page after page. Half an hour later, Chet, nodding in a chair, suddenly became aware of a figure moving behind the stacks about ten feet from the spot where he sat. Instantly he was wide awake.

He leaped out of his chair, and dashed toward the eavesdropper. A sudden beam of light through the stacks revealed the identity of the intruder.

"Benny Tass!" Chet cried.

With Chet after him the bully raced out the door, slamming it in Chet's face.

"Tail him, Chet!" Frank ordered.

With Joe posted at the door, the others continued to try the improvised sheet over the pages of several books. Nothing that indicated a message turned up.

"I guess I didn't get the layout right," Greg said finally in disgust. "It looks as though we're on a wild-goose chase!"

"You can't be sure," Frank told him encouragingly. "Maybe we just haven't found the right book. We're not going to stop until we've gone through every book this size."

They had just started on another volume when Chet burst in. He was red-faced and excited.

"First Benny went to see Kurt in his office!" he finally managed to say. "Benny didn't shut the door tight. They talked for a long time. Then through the crack I saw Kurt take a sealed envelope from his pocket. Without another word he handed it to Benny, who came out. I hid so he didn't see me."

"Where's Benny now?" Frank asked.

"He just ran out the front door and jumped into his car. I heard him tell someone he was driving to Bayport."

"Let's follow him!" Frank cried to Joe.

The Hardys hurried from the building and raced off in their convertible in pursuit!

CHAPTER X

A Puzzling Ad

IT seemed as if Benny had wings on his car. He sped over the country road at a reckless pace, and only because Frank handled the convertible with the skill of a racing driver was he able to keep the other car in sight.

When Benny hit the downtown area and ran into a series of traffic lights, he proceeded at a more reasonable rate of speed.

"Do you think he knows we're following him?" Frank mused as he drove along about a block behind Benny.

"Doesn't act like it," Joe answered. "He'd be turning corners, trying to lose us."

Benny was taking the most direct route toward the center of town. He drove into the main business section, found a parking place, and hopped out of his car.

"He's going into the office of the *Bayport Times*," Frank noted with interest.

"That envelope Kurt gave him must be for someone in there," Joe surmised.

Before the Hardys had time to trail Benny into the building, he reappeared, got into his car, and drove speedily away.

"Shall we follow him back?" Joe asked.

Frank shook his head. "I think it would be better to find out what he was doing."

In the newspaper office they found that the clerk on duty was a portly old gentleman they knew well.

"Well, if it isn't the Hardy boys," Mr. Brown greeted them. "What are you two sleuths up to now?"

"We're looking for a little information," Frank answered.

"I suppose you're working on a case. Well, what can I do for you?"

"Just a minute ago," Frank explained, "a heavy-set fellow came in here with an envelope. Could you tell us which department it went to?"

"The envelope contained an ad."

"What did the ad say?" Frank queried.

"Now that"—Mr. Brown chuckled—"I can't tell you. It would be against the paper's rules. But I guess it wouldn't hurt to tell you that it was a Personal." Then he added, "Even if I dared let you know what it said, I couldn't, because I sent it right through." He tapped a delivery chute alongside him.

The Hardys thanked Mr. Brown for the information and returned to their car.

"At least we know where to look when we check tomorrow's paper," Joe said hopefully.

"Let's stop home and get the cutout sheet of paper that Kurt left with Dad," Frank remarked as he swung the car from the curb. "We can say hello to Mother and Aunt Gertrude and pick up some fresh clothes."

Upon reaching their house, the boys received the usual friendly reprimands from Aunt Gertrude.

Mrs. Hardy looked at her sons, an anxious expression in her eyes. "I can't help feeling concerned when you're at the Academy. Especially since your father's warning of danger there."

The boys smiled reassuringly at their mother, and promised that they would take no unnecessary chances. Just then Aunt Gertrude called that a snack was ready.

After they had eaten, they changed their clothing and stowed a few extra things in an overnight bag. As they started back to the Academy, Frank patted his jacket pocket to make sure that the folded paper of rectangular cutouts, which he had taken from his father's desk, was still there.

"It will be interesting to see how this sheet compares with the one that Greg made this afternoon," he said to Joe. "Even if it should be a fake, as Dad suspects, the difference between it and the one Greg made might provide a clue."

"Maybe so, but the idea of looking through all those books in the library again makes me want to scream." Joe groaned.

Back at the school, they found that Chet and Greg were in a double room next to theirs. Greg was getting ready for bed. Chet, head propped up on three pillows, was reading a magazine.

"What happened?" he demanded.

Briefly, the Hardys recounted the chase which had led to the newspaper office. Then Frank produced Kurt's sheet of cutouts and checked it against the one Greg had made.

"They're certainly different," Greg observed. He was eager to try Kurt's copy on the library books.

Frank suggested that Joe go to bed. "You've had a rough day," he said.

"Guess I could use some shut-eye," Joe admitted.

Chet yawned. "How about me? I'm bushed, too, making meals for a hungry wolf pack all day long."

Frank grinned. "Okay. And listen, in the morning I'll have breakfast in bed, sausage, pancakes, plenty of syrup."

"And coffee with a yellow feather," Chet said as he rolled over to go to sleep.

Frank and Greg, armed with flashlights, tiptoed down the deserted corridor carrying both copies of the cutouts. They entered the library and closed the door behind them. There was not a sound but the ticking of the old-fashioned clock on the wall. Its hands stood at midnight.

The two settled themselves at a large table. With the aid of their flashlights they re-examined many of the books they had checked earlier that evening, trying to find a clue in the difference between the two sheets. For more than an hour they looked for a combination of words that made sense.

Finally Frank gave up. "I think it's hopeless," he said. "And we still don't know if Dad is right about Kurt's sheet being a fake."

Greg yawned. "We have no guarantee that mine is correct, either. I've got a pretty good memory, but who knows? I might have left something out, or moved one of the cutouts either to the left or right of its designated place. Well, let's head for bed."

Frank followed him out of the library.

Their eyes accustomed to the darkness, the boys moved silently through the wing. Just before they reached the main part of the building, Frank suddenly stopped short.

"*Sss-s-t!* Greg—wait—"

Frank was staring upward at the frosted-glass transom of one of the classrooms.

"What's up?" Greg whispered.

"I'm sure I saw a light flickering in there!"

Frank gripped the knob and flung open the door. Almost with the same motion, his other hand found the switch for the overhead light. Illumination flooded the room.

A man in a dressing gown, his back to them, stood in the middle of two rows of desks. He was holding a small flashlight and seemed frozen into immobility. But in a second he turned.

"Mr. Kurt!" Greg and Frank cried.

The headmaster glared at them balefully. "Why are you wandering about at this hour?" he thundered.

"We saw a light in here," Frank explained, "and came to see who the burglar was."

"I'm just inspecting the classrooms," Kurt explained testily, walking toward them. "You needn't trouble yourselves by snooping."

On a hunch Frank moved quickly toward the spot where Kurt was standing. Casually he glanced down at the nearest desk.

Crudely carved into its polished surface was:

REVENGE HARRIS D.

Kurt, apparently upset that Frank had seen the strange message carved into the desk, tugged nervously at his beard.

"Who was Harris D?" Frank inquired.

"I don't know," Kurt snorted.

Frank looked hard at Kurt to see if the man

were withholding information, but the head-master did not flicker an eyelid.

He urged Frank and Greg into the hall and on toward their rooms. In the morning Frank told Joe what had happened.

"There must be something very important in that classroom," his brother remarked. "What could it be?"

"It certainly is related to that desk," Frank answered as he pulled on his sweater. "Kurt was pretty eager to get us away from it."

"Let's take another look," Joe suggested.

The Hardys finished dressing and hurried to-ward the classroom. The corridor was deserted. Employing caution, however, Joe remained at the door while Frank crossed to the carved desk.

"Someone has removed the top!" Frank called. "There's a brand-new one here now!"

"I'm sure Harris D is the answer," Joe as-serted. "If we can find him, he might give us a clue."

The boys decided to work on this new angle as soon as possible. But first they wanted to get the paper and check the Personal ads.

As they walked out of the classroom and along the hallway, they met Mr. Teevan with several copies of the *Bayport Times* under his arm.

"Good morning," Frank said. "We were just going out for the paper. Can we borrow one of yours?"

"Sure. You can keep it."

"How is your wife?" Joe asked.

"Tolerably well," the custodian answered. "She hasn't got over her fright completely. But I dare say she'll be back at work in a day or two. Well, good-by, boys."

"So long. And thanks for the paper."

Frank and Joe bounded up the stairs to the guest room. Frank spread the *Times* on the dresser and turned to the Personal column. Quickly he ran his finger down the advertisements. As he neared the bottom of the list, he gave a shout.

Just then Greg and Chet walked in.

"Listen to this!" Frank said excitedly. " '*Yellow Feather: Meet 100 F.R. Pt. 2101.*' "

"Wow!" Chet exclaimed. "That must be the ad Kurt put in!"

"He might have done it to send us on some wild-goose chase," Joe suggested. "I'm convinced that he'd go to great lengths to get rid of us."

"In which case you won't move a step away from here!" Chet said firmly.

"I think we should follow up the clue, even if it's a trap. Since we know it might be, we can be prepared," Frank said.

"But what does that code mean?" Chet asked, repeating the words. "There's no doubt about the Yellow Feather part. But what about the rest?"

"One hundred F.R. Pt.," Frank said. "One

hundred what? Feet maybe? One hundred feet R. Pt."

"Rocky Point on Barmet Bay!" Chet exclaimed.

"A meeting place," Greg agreed. "Sounds logical."

"The rest is easy," Joe said. "Two thousand, one hundred and one. Twenty-one 0 one. The naval and military way of telling time. Twenty-one means nine P.M., and the 0 one means one minute after nine."

"Meet one hundred feet off Rocky Point at one minute past nine P.M.," Frank read the complete message. "As I said before, it could be a trap. But it could also be a meeting between our buddy and the Yellow Feather. If so, we'll have to catch them in the act!"

"In the *Sleuth?*" his brother asked, referring to their sleek motorboat.

"No," Frank corrected him. "We'd be smarter not to take our own boat—someone might be watching for us to start out in it and follow us."

"Then how about Tony Prito?" Joe suggested. "He says his *Napoli* is in good shape and I know he'll be glad to take us."

"Good idea," Frank said.

"Well, I hope you don't want me to go," Chet spoke up. "Operation Sub-zero—*br-r-r!*"

The Hardys looked at Greg. "Joe and I should do this job alone," Frank said. "I'd hate to expose you to danger. Anyway, both you fellows ought to stay here and keep your eyes open."

After breakfast Frank called Tony Prito. The star end of Bayport High's football team and close friend of the Hardys was always ready for adventure. He assured Frank that he would be delighted to take them out.

"Meet me at eight o'clock," he told them. "Drive out Shore Road, and I'll have the *Napoli* waiting for you in Segram's Cove."

Frank had just stepped from the booth when a familiar voice called:

"Hi, Frank!"

"Skinny! Say, you're just the person I need."

"Swell. What can I do for you?"

"Play detective. Find Benny Tass and ask how he got permission to go to Bayport last night. Tell him you heard that he was seen there at the newspaper office. Report to me how he reacts and what he says."

Skinny said he would do it at once. But as he started off, another thought came to Frank and he called him back.

"Did you ever hear of an alumnus of Woodson Academy called Harris D?" he asked.

Skinny's forehead wrinkled. "Harris D— Would you mean Harris Dilleau by any chance?"

"Maybe. Who was he and when was he here?"

"Why, a long time ago. I've heard my uncle John Mason talk about him several times. He was in the same class. Uncle John graduated about twenty-two years ago."

"What did he say about Dilleau?" Frank was intensely interested.

"Oh, he was a real troublemaker, my uncle said. I think he was expelled from school."

The boys separated and Frank went to the guest room to relay this latest bit of information to Joe.

"Now we're getting somewhere!" Joe cried. "Let's go to the library and see if we can find out anything more about Dilleau in the yearbooks."

But as they scanned the row of annuals, they became discouraged. There was only one publication which dealt with Dilleau's years at Woodson. Although Skinny's uncle was mentioned prominently, there was only one short reference to Harris D.

Joe returned the volume to its proper place. "I'm going to search for the missing yearbooks," he declared, "and see if they contain any information about Dilleau. I'll bet he's a friend of Kurt."

During the day he examined shelf after shelf of books but drew a blank. Frank busied himself trailing Kurt. The headmaster's activities, however, were above suspicion.

Skinny Mason came to Frank later in the afternoon to report on Benny Tass. The boy had admitted to him that he had gone to the *Bayport Times* with an advertisement, but claimed it had not appeared in that day's paper.

Frank and Joe did not believe Benny's story. And when they set out that evening they were thinking as much about Kurt as the Yellow Feather, hoping to capture both of them.

They drove to Segram's Cove by a circuitous route in order to throw off any possible followers, but reached the bay shore at exactly eight o'clock.

Frank cast the car headlights over the water and the beams picked out Tony in his motorboat. Frank turned off the lights, locked the car, and the boys started down the slippery embankment.

The sound of an engine reached their ears as the boat drew toward them, then they heard Tony's voice as the bow of the *Napoli* scraped softly against the low dock. An instant later he was running up the snowy slope to meet them.

"Hi, Tony," Frank greeted their friend. "Good timing, eh?"

"Good timing, but bad conditions. Frank, I don't think we can go. There's too much floating ice in the bay!"

ST. JOHN THE BAPTIST PARISH LIBRARY
2920 NEW HIGHWAY 51
LAPLACE, LOUISIANA 70068

CHAPTER XI

Dangerous Waters

"You mean we'll have to give up an opportunity to capture the Yellow Feather?" Frank asked with a groan of disappointment.

"Tony," Joe said, "this might be our only chance!"

The *Napoli*'s skipper shrugged. "The whole bay is full of great chunks of ice. If we hit one of those floes, it would knock a hole in the hull so fast we'd sink like a rock."

Through the darkness, the boys could see the white floes bobbing up and down on the water.

"Miniature icebergs," Frank observed. "But I sure hate to miss this opportunity of perhaps solving the mystery."

"I'll tell you what," Tony spoke up. "I'm willing to risk the boat. You fellows pilot her. You're better navigators than I am."

"I'm game if you are!" Frank cried, and Joe agreed.

All three sprinted out on the dock and jumped into the *Napoli*.

"You take the wheel, Frank," Joe said, then released the line.

Frank assured Tony he would use care and eased the sleek craft out into the ice-jammed water. Since he did not wish to betray their presence, he decided to proceed without lights.

"Joe, crawl onto the bow and tell me where to steer," he directed.

Joe felt his way forward in the dark. Lying on the deck with his head hanging over the prow, he kept up a rapid-fire series of instructions.

"Who would ever keep an appointment out here in the bay on a night like this?" Tony asked as the *Napoli* snaked slowly among the chunks of ice.

"I don't know, except the Yellow Feather!" Frank said.

As the boat moved farther out of the cove, the danger from the ice increased.

"Frank, port, hard!" Joe commanded.

Desperately Frank spun the wheel. There was a slight scraping along the starboard gunwale, and a gasp of relief from Joe, as an ominous section of ice floated astern.

"How far off Rocky Point are we, Tony?" Frank asked, peering into the darkness.

"We must be getting close. Maybe you'd better cut her down some. You can almost drift in."

"See anything ahead there, Joe?" Frank called in a low voice.

"Not a thing."

In a few minutes they were in the shadow of sheer rocks of the Point that towered menacingly. The *Napoli* was crawling now. Joe kept a constant watch for ice, while Tony searched the sea for the shadowy outline of another craft.

Suddenly there was the sharp *boi-i-ng* whine of a projectile near their heads! Instinctively the boys ducked. *Splash!* The object struck the water ten feet from the craft.

"Where'd that come from?" Joe called.

Neither Frank nor Tony could answer.

Before the boat had gone twenty yards there was another whine. This time all three felt a convulsive shudder jar the boat. The *Napoli* had been hit!

"Look at this!" Tony cried.

The tip of a small harpoon was embedded in the wood of the boat about a foot above the water line. Tony wrenched the missile loose and pulled it into the cockpit.

"Holy crow!" Joe exclaimed. "Let's get out of here quick."

Frank spun hard to starboard and the *Napoli* lurched seaward. A second later there came another twang, followed by a splash sending a spout of water high into the air directly in front of them.

"We're in a trap!" Frank exclaimed. "Our only chance is to hide!"

Pulling on the wheel frantically, he headed the boat back toward the protection of the rocks.

"Frank! Ice!" Joe warned him.

Blocking their course to the safe shelter of the Point was what looked like a flotilla of ice floes! Frank realized that it would be almost impossible to steer through them. Desperately he searched for an escape route. He saw only one possible way out of their hazardous situation.

"Joe! Come back here!" he called.

At the same time he cut the throttle, spinning the wheel first one way, then the other, so that the *Napoli* course made the boat a difficult target.

Joe crawled back along the deck and jumped to his brother's side. Quickly Frank related his plan. Instantly Joe grabbed a boat hook and slid up to the bow again. At the same time Frank cupped his hands to his mouth and yelled at the top of his lungs:

"Help! We're sinking! Save us!"

Then he steered the speedboat toward an overhanging cliff, and under the jutting cover. With the boat hook Joe kept her from bouncing against the rocks.

The boys waited, but there were no more *twangs* of death-dealing harpoons. The ruse had worked!

"Where do you suppose the harpoons were fired from?" Tony whispered.

"They seemed to come out of nowhere," Joe replied in a low voice. "I didn't even hear the sound of a gun firing them, did you?"

"No," the others answered.

"What puzzles me," Frank mused, "is those funny *twang* sounds we heard just before the harpoons landed."

"Hold it!" Joe demanded. "Listen!"

In the crash of surf and the whistle of wind they heard another sound.

"A motorboat!" Frank said hoarsely.

The unseen craft was evidently speeding toward them. The noise grew louder with every second.

"Do you suppose he knows we're here?" Tony asked fearfully. "If not, there's going to be a crash!"

"Let's move," Joe suggested.

"But where? We don't dare show ourselves," Frank objected. "I say, take a chance and stay here."

The boat continued on in their direction at breakneck speed.

"This is it!" Joe announced tersely as the other craft did not swerve. "Get ready for a fight with the Yellow Feather!"

They waited tensely while the sound of the approaching motor came closer. Then the outline of another speedboat took form in the darkness, zigzagging about fifty yards off their starboard side.

"It's searching for us!" Frank whispered.

The craft was almost abreast when a waterspout seemed to rise directly in front of it.

"She's being fired on, too!" Joe cried.

The boat practically jumped from the sea as its skipper gave it the gun. But even as he did, another big splash rose alongside the craft.

By this time it was evident to the Hardys that the harpoons were coming from the high rocks of the Point rather than from a craft.

"Whoever's in that boat is going to make a run for it!" Frank stated.

"Why don't we make our break now, too?" Joe suggested. "Two boats out there will divide the target."

"Okay," Frank agreed. "Besides, I want to see who's in that boat."

He started the motor and waved Joe to let go with his grappling hook. The *Napoli* streaked forward, angling from left to right.

"We'll be out of range in a minute!" Frank yelled. "Then we'll take off after that other boat."

The boys heard one more big splash behind them, then the attacks stopped. The pilot of the craft ahead had opened up and ripped off in a straight course toward Bayport.

"That fellow can really handle a boat," Tony remarked as they watched him cut between ice floes without losing speed or direction.

Frank tailed the other craft. But in spite of the wide-open throttle and a path to follow, he could not gain on it.

"We'd better let him go before we crack up the *Napoli!*" Frank said. "How about my taking her into your boathouse, Tony, instead of Segram's Cove? That hole the harpoon made ought to be checked right away."

"Okay. I'll drive you back in my jalopy to pick up your car," Tony suggested.

At the boathouse the boys used a block and tackle rigged to an electric motor, and hauled the *Napoli* up on rollers to examine the damage.

"Not as bad as I thought," Tony said.

"I'm relieved," said Frank. "Just the same it will cost something to fix. Joe and I will pay for it."

Tony would not agree to this, and the Hardys could not change his mind.

"It's all in the cause of detective work," he said.

"Well, at least let us help you patch it. Got any stuff here?"

"No."

"We have some in our boathouse," Joe said.

"Okay," Tony said. "Let's get it and I'll make the repairs tomorrow."

The three boys hurried to the Hardy boathouse, which was not far from Tony's. Frank unlocked the door and switched on the light. The trim *Sleuth* gleamed in her berth.

"Hey, she's wet!" Joe cried suddenly. He jumped in and felt the motor. "Why, she's just been used!"

The next instant Tony groaned. "There's a small hole in her side just like the one the harpoon put in the *Napoli!*"

The boys looked at one another in consternation.

"Listen, if those crooks think they can steal our own boat to chase us in—" Joe began.

Suddenly Frank burst into laughter. Tony and Joe stared at him in amazement.

"I think I know whom we were chasing." Frank chuckled. "Detective Fenton Hardy!"

"What! Your dad?" Tony gasped.

"No wonder he outmaneuvered us," Joe said, grinning. "Dad's the only one I know who handles a boat that well."

Frank laughed. "Will we give him a cross-examination!"

He quickly found the calking material and handed it to Tony.

"Thanks," Tony said. "I know you fellows want to get home, so I'll drive you to your car."

A little while later Joe slid behind the wheel of the convertible and drove home.

Bursting into the living room, they found their father in lounging jacket and slippers before the fireplace. He was reading an FBI report.

"Nice night for a boat ride, wasn't it, Dad?" Frank queried.

The boys eagerly watched their father's face, but he only raised his eyebrows questioningly. Joe touched the detective's tousled hair.

"Um, damp," he said. "Couldn't be from the salt spray, could it?"

The corners of Mr. Hardy's mouth crinkled and he broke into a hearty laugh. "All right, you win!"

"And what were you doing out in the bay?" Frank asked.

"Well, I happened to notice the ad about the Yellow Feather in today's paper," Mr. Hardy explained, "and called the school to ask if you had seen it. When Chet told me where you'd gone, I decided you might need some help."

Frank told his father about trailing Benny to the *Times* office, and the discovery of the advertisement.

"Well," Mr. Hardy said, "the code was rather easy to figure out. That made me think that it was a plant."

"We suspected it, too, But by whom? The Yellow Feather?"

"Possibly. In any case it was designed to put us off the case for good!"

"Dad, now that we know Kurt is tied up in this do you think he could be the Yellow Feather?" Frank asked.

"Until I have more proof, I'll reserve judgment. I do believe, though, that he's trying to steal the Woodson estate from Greg, and perhaps old Elias was afraid of him."

"Was that the reason you called Mother about us being in danger?" Frank wanted to know.

"Yes. We must get back the original cutout paper which Greg lost," Mr. Hardy declared.

Joe told of his suspicions that Henry Kurt might keep it locked in his office filing cabinet.

"I saw him take out a sheet of paper and put it in his pocket," Joe went on. "Maybe when he's alone he tries to figure out what the cutouts mean."

"That's very likely," his father said. "I think that Kurt made the one he left with me as a cover-up for his own underhanded work."

After talking to Mr. Hardy a while longer, the boys said good night and took off for the Academy. They were halfway along the winding country road when Joe noticed a peculiar reflection in the sky.

"Looks like a fire," he said. "Frank! Do you suppose it's at the school?"

CHAPTER XII

A Disastrous Fire

FRANK gave the car the gun and the convertible roared along the road. He braked to a stop at the edge of a field that bordered the campus.

Before them an immense bonfire was sending flames high into the air. In its flickering light was a group of excited students.

"Say, what's this?" Frank murmured, jumping from the car.

"There's Skinny and Chet," Joe said.

"And Benny," Frank added, almost bumping into the bully. "What's going on, Tass?"

"Semester celebration! We don't have to go to bed until we want to. It was Kurt's idea. He gave us a lot of old record books to burn up."

"*Record books?* He can't do that!" Frank cried in dismay. He whispered to Joe, "If those records are destroyed, we'll never find out anything about Harris Dilleau!"

112

The Hardys ran over to Chet and took him aside. "Where's Greg?" Joe asked. "He'd better order the boys to stop this!"

"Greg's gone," Chet replied. "He received a message calling him back to college."

Realizing that there was no time to lose if the records were to be saved, Frank leaped between the fire and the students.

"Fellows!" he cried. "We have to put out this fire! Important papers are being burned. Grab all the snow you can hold and throw it on the flames!"

But before the boys could carry out his order, Benny jumped forward and shouted, "Bunk! Why should we put it out just because you say so? It's been a long time since we had a fire like this!"

"There are valuable records in there," Frank retorted. "We must save them!"

He leaped to a nearby snowbank and swept up an armload of snow. As he turned to throw it on the fire, the bulky figure of Benny Tass blocked his path.

"Look out, Frank!"

Joe's warning shout cut through the hubbub of excited students, but it came too late.

Frank did not see Benny's foot, which the bully had stuck out deliberately to trip him. The young detective sprawled headfirst toward the fire.

Like a cat, Joe pounced after his brother and

grabbed his coat. He pulled Frank clear of the blaze before it had time to ignite his clothing, then helped him to his feet.

"Is he all right?" Skinny cried, seeing Frank's blackened face.

Anxiously everyone gazed at the unfortunate boy, who rubbed his face with his glove. The only apparent injury was a pair of singed eyebrows.

Chet angrily faced Benny. "That was a dirty trick," he said. "You tripped him on purpose!"

The students gathered around, sensing a fight.

"It was an accident," Benny declared as Chet doubled up his fists. "I'm sorry."

Despite his apology, the onlookers stared at one another in disbelief. A few minutes previously, most of the students had been ready to side with Tass. Now the entire group turned against him.

"Let's put out that fire as Frank said!" one of them shouted.

Before Benny could protest, the boys began to throw snow on the flames.

"Here's a fire extinguisher," cried Skinny, who had run to the school's garage to get it.

Between the extinguisher and the snow heaped on the giant blaze, it soon died down. Chet, meanwhile, had hurried off to the tool shed and soon returned with two steel rakes. Joe grabbed one. Together they pried into the sodden mass, yanking out what was left of the record books.

"Oh, good night!" Joe moaned in dismay. "The fire extinguisher liquid has messed up what the fire didn't."

The pages of the book he had picked showed only blurred, washed-out traces of ink.

"Maybe not all of them are ruined," Frank said hopefully, and the raking went on.

Several students helped, using their glove-protected hands. Soon there was a mass of partly charred papers stacked up in the snow.

Off to one side, Benny Tass was still complaining bitterly. "It's a fine thing," he blustered, "when we let a couple of smart alecks from town come on the campus and tell us we can't have a celebration!"

Most of the boys ignored him, but his few close buddies stood by him.

"Hey," exclaimed one of Tass's pals, "Here comes Mr. Kurt. Wait till he hears about this."

The headmaster stomped onto the scene. Immediately Benny told him how the Hardys had ordered the fire doused. Kurt stormed over to where the boys were still trying to salvage some of the records.

"What's the idea?" he barked. "I gave permission for that bonfire."

Frank stepped up to the headmaster. "Mr. Kurt, you know as well as I do that Gregory Woodson wouldn't want any records of this school burned."

"But I'm the one who is in charge here," Kurt said pompously.

"I'd like to remind you," Frank replied, "that Greg Woodson has been named by the court as administrator of his grandfather's estate. The school and its records are a valuable part of that estate."

Kurt was speechless with rage.

"The destruction of the records could turn out to be a criminal offense!" Joe added.

Kurt finally found his voice. "I looked over all the records. There wasn't anything valuable in them." After a slight pause he said threateningly, "You Hardys will regret this. No one can come in here and tamper with my authority!"

"No one's trying to do that," Frank said. "But we're going to save Woodson Academy for its rightful owner."

At a murmur from the students, Kurt suddenly realized that he had lost face with them. Purple with rage he stalked off, ordering his young charges to follow him. From a distance the Hardys and Chet could hear him trying to explain his side of the case.

The unpleasant scene over, the boys returned to their salvage work. Soon every readable scrap had been gathered up into a small pile.

"I sure hope there's a clue to this mystery in here to make our work worthwhile," Chet puffed. "Maybe Kurt was right."

"I think just the opposite might be true," Frank spoke up. "They might contain items he doesn't want us to see. If only those particular ones didn't burn or weren't ruined by the fire extinguisher."

Joe spoke up, "Kurt probably gave the telltale ones to the boys first. They would have been on the bottom of the pile."

"And were saved!" Chet chortled, his enthusiasm returning. "Say, fellows, we ought to hide these papers so Kurt can't find them."

"Or the Yellow Feather or Tass," Joe agreed.

"We could take them to your room," said Chet, then chuckled. "But after the way Frank's trousers wound up on top of the bell tower, I wouldn't say it's a safe place."

"I know," said Frank. "Let's hide the papers in the tool shed. Unless we're spotted moving them in, no one would think of looking in there."

Making sure that nobody was in sight, the boys split the pile of charred records into three armloads and carried them to the shed.

By the light of a lantern which they found, they stacked them in a corner and covered them with a tarpaulin. The Hardys would investigate the contents in the morning. Frank had found a padlock with a key which he was about to snap on the door when Chet spoke up.

"I have a better idea. One of us really ought to guard these papers. You fellows must be dead tired after all you've been through today, so I'll stay."

"Okay," Frank said. "You're a real pal."

With Chet inside the shed, he locked the door and departed quickly with Joe for their room.

Chet relighted the lantern and set it on a workbench. Then he decided to begin looking in the pile of records for clues.

One by one, he began going through the papers. The stack of discarded possibilities was growing high when Chet found an interesting item.

"Boy oh boy!" he murmured.

At the same instant he became aware of a scraping sound outside the shed. Quickly extinguishing the lantern he peered out the window. It was so dark he could see nothing at first. But as his eyes adjusted themselves to the change, some of the blackness took shape. It seemed to be moving!

As Chet watched, terrified, the moving object became a person. Was he heading for the tool shed?

Instinctively the youth started to drop out of sight, in case a light should be flashed in his direction. Before he got below the level of the sill, there was a crash of glass and something hit him full force on the head.

Chet sagged to the floor.

CHAPTER XIII

A Minor Explosion

EARLY the next morning Frank and Joe hopped out of bed and dressed quickly.

"I wonder how Chet made out last night," Frank mused as they hurried toward the tool shed, first making sure that no one was following them.

Joe grinned as they neared the tool house. "We'll probably find him lying sound asleep smack on top of the records!"

Suddenly both boys uttered cries of alarm. Crudely painted on the side of the shed was a large yellow feather! Fearful now that something might have happened to Chet, the Hardys raced forward. Getting closer, they saw the broken window. A second later a bound and gagged figure rose into view.

Chet Morton!

The prisoner's hair was disheveled and there was a smear of blood on one cheek.

"That Yellow Feather is a fiend!" Frank exclaimed as he hastily unlocked the door and rushed inside.

He removed Chet's gag while Joe cut the bonds that held his friend's arms.

"For Pete's sake!" Frank said. "What happened? And are you all right?"

"Guess so. I was conked," Chet replied, rubbing a bruise over his left ear. "Somebody shot at me. I went out like a light."

"Say," said Joe, bending down to pick something off the floor, "I'll bet this is what hit you!"

In his hand was a small dart. It was about six inches long and had a leather-covered knob at one end.

"The kind that can be fired from a gun!" Frank cried excitedly. Then another thought struck him. "Chet, the records!"

"They're—they're gone," Chet said dejectedly.

Joe leaped to the corner in which the papers had been stacked the night before and groaned. "All our work for nothing!"

"We really have been taken in by the Yellow Feather," Frank said as he turned to Chet. "Tell us exactly what happened."

Chet related all he could remember.

"I didn't see the person well enough to identify him," he said ruefully. "But he sure fixed me up."

"You seem to be all right now," Joe remarked.

"Maybe even a little fatter, as a matter of fact!"

"Say, I'm not so—" Chet began, patting his midriff. "Oh, I almost forgot!"

Grinning as he unbuttoned his jacket, he brought out a thick record book which had been hidden against his stomach.

"I was going through the papers," he explained. "I had just come across this book when I heard the noise, so I stuck it under my coat. Dilleau's name is in it," Chet added proudly.

"Great work!" Joe said, and Frank praised, "Chet, you're an ace!"

"Some of the stuff about Dilleau was washed out by the fire-extinguisher liquid," Chet went on, "but part of it's left."

"Never mind, we'll take the records to our lab and try to restore them by special chemical treatment," Joe said enthusiastically.

Overjoyed that something had been saved, the Hardys took the charred book from the shed, locked it in the trunk of their car, and returned to the school. To their surprise, Mrs. Teevan was back and breakfast was ready. As they headed for the dining hall, the boys met Greg Woodson.

"That phone call requesting me to go back to college was a fake!" he informed them. "I'd sure like to know who sent me on that wild-goose chase."

"Kurt might have done it to get you out of the way while he was having a lot of old records burned," Frank said, and told Greg about the "celebration."

"Well, he won't catch me off guard again," Greg said firmly. "I'm sticking right here!"

After breakfast Frank told him that he and Joe planned to go home to work in their laboratory and try to restore the old data about Dilleau. Chet said he would leave too.

When the Hardys climbed into their car, Frank could not get any response from the motor.

"The fuel gauge!" he exclaimed, pointing to the *empty* reading. "But I filled the tank yesterday!"

"Somebody must have siphoned off the gas," Joe surmised. "Maybe we can borrow another car."

When they tried to start Greg's car they discovered that it, too, had no gas.

"Someone doesn't want us to leave here," Frank said. "First he doesn't want us to stay, now he doesn't want us to go."

"Maybe the Yellow Feather found out that we wanted to restore the records about Harris Dilleau," Joe suggested.

"All the more reason for us getting to our lab as fast as possible," Frank said. "But how?"

Joe grinned, then mentioned Chet's new contraption. It was better than walking! Taking the records from the car trunk, they went to find their pal.

"So you want another ride on my propeller sled?" Chet grinned. But upon learning that the Hardys' car and Greg's had been drained of fuel, he sobered. "Come on," he said. "We'll outsmart the Yellow Feather yet."

The three boys hurried to the river where Chet's invention was lashed to the school dock. Frank and Joe began to slip the lines that held it secure, and Chet spun the flywheel.

Boom!

The concussion of the explosion nearly knocked all three of them over. As they regained their balance, Frank asked, "What happened?"

Still a little groggy, Chet started to examine his motorized sled.

"The muffler," he said in a sorrowful voice, "has been blown to bits."

Parts of the cylindrical noise absorber were scattered over a wide area of ice.

"Someone put an explosive mixture in it," Chet groaned. "Benny Tass, I'll bet."

Chet wound the rope around the flywheel again and tugged. To his amazement, the motor caught hold and burst into a throaty roar.

"We may be driven deaf, but I'll get you fellows to Bayport," he yelled. "Climb aboard."

Once they picked up speed, the noise seemed to lessen.

"I'd sure like to know who wrecked my muffler," Chet grumbled. "Maybe it wasn't Benny after all. Kurt's mad enough at all of us to have done it."

As Joe remarked that he doubted that the headmaster would stoop to anything so childish, Frank's thoughts about the man were concentrating along other lines. Finally he said:

"You know, Skinny Mason once told us that Kurt was an expert on spring propulsion. I'd forgotten about it until now. I wonder if that dart which knocked you out, Chet—"

"You mean he has invented some kind of noiseless pistol to fire darts?" Chet exploded.

"Exactly. And a large one that sent those harpoons out on the bay. That would account for the funny *twang* we heard," Frank said.

Since the Morton farm was nearer than the Hardys' home, Chet planned to go there, then drive Frank and Joe to their house in his father's car. Two pretty girls opened the door for them.

"It's about time," Callie and Iola chorused in mock severity. "We've been waiting for you!"

"What's doing?" Joe grinned at Iola.

"Have you forgotten that tonight's the big sleigh ride?" she demanded.

"We were so tied up with this Yellow Feather mystery we never gave it a thought," he said apologetically.

"Well, we have it all arranged," Callie said.

"Old Mr. Kemper is going to take us." And then the girls told of the plans they had made.

"If we're going on a sleigh ride"—Frank finally broke in—"Joe and I had better get home fast and do some work."

The Hardys departed, with Chet driving them in the Morton car.

At their house Frank and Joe were greeted in the hall by a peppery voice:

"Well, it's a pity you're never around when you're wanted!"

"Hello, Aunt Gertrude." Joe laughed. "Maybe we ought to have cards printed—*At Home Tuesdays!*"

"It would be a fine idea," his aunt snapped. "Then a visitor would know when to find you."

"Visitor? Did we have a visitor?" Frank asked seriously.

"Yes, indeed, but he couldn't wait. I gave him what he came for. He said to tell you that Benny Tass had been here."

CHAPTER XIV

The Wild Chase

"BENNY TASS!" Frank exclaimed. "What did he want?"

"Benny wanted the Woodson Academy annual for the year in which your father was graduated. He explained to me that there was no copy of that yearbook at school."

"But what was his reason?" Joe asked.

"The boy explained that he was writing a story for the school's monthly bulletin about famous Woodson athletes. Your father was one of the best that ever played in sports there, so naturally some facts about him should be included."

"Did you give him the book?" Frank asked.

"Why, certainly! Would you want your father's name omitted from a story like that?"

Frank had to agree on that point but added, "I'm not sure Benny gave you the real reason he wanted to get his hands on Dad's yearbook."

Aunt Gertrude bristled. "You mean he wasn't telling the truth?"

The boys told her of their search to make the strange cutout sheets fit various book pages to reveal an important message.

"Kurt probably sent Benny here," Frank said. "We don't trust those two. Kurt may have found out that the message is in Dad's yearbook!"

"Well get going," Aunt Gertrude cried, "and bring that yearbook back before your father comes home!"

As the boys ran toward the garage for Mr. Hardy's car, Joe said, "Now I'm sure it was Benny who drained the gas out of our car. He didn't want us to get here before he did!"

"Right."

A few seconds later the motor purred to life and the boys started off. Frank drove as fast as he dared on the snow-packed roads.

Minutes later Joe cried excitedly, "There's a car up ahead! It might be Benny's!"

Foot by foot, they gained on the other vehicle. Obviously its driver did not realize that he was being pursued, otherwise he might have put on more speed.

"It's Tass, all right!" Joe said gleefully as they neared the car ahead.

"I'm going to force him to the side and make him stop," Frank said.

He pulled up in back of Benny and then swung

alongside him. When the bully saw the Hardys, he made a desperate effort to get away, giving his motor full power. But the acceleration was fatal on the snowy road, and as his wheels spun wildly, Frank edged in front of him, forcing the youth to stop.

"What's the big idea?" Benny yelled angrily as the Hardys hopped out and strode over to him.

"You have Dad's yearbook," Joe answered. "We want it back."

"Your aunt lent it to me," Benny snapped. "Isn't that good enough for you?"

"No, it's not," Frank said coldly. "Hand it over, Benny—right now."

"Wait a second, will you?" The bully dropped his blustering tone a little. "We just want to get some material out of it, that's all."

"Who's we?" Frank inquired.

"Why, Kurt. He's going to read it."

"Nothing doing," Joe insisted. "Give it to me, Benny."

For a moment the bully fumed, his face red with anger. Then he decided there was nothing he could do with the odds against him but return the borrowed annual.

"Okay, if that's the way you feel about it," he said in a surly tone.

With that he picked up the book from the seat and started to hand it over. But as Joe reached through the window to take it, Benny's other hand flashed to the dashboard. In one movement he yanked out the ashtray full of cigarette refuse and emptied it into Joe's face! With a yelp of pain the boy fell back, trying to wipe the ashes from his eyes.

Benny, with a clashing of gears, gunned his motor.

"Oh, no, you don't!" Frank cried and dived through the window to take control.

One twist of the steering wheel and the car was off the road and on the soft shoulder in deep snow. Then Frank snapped off the ignition.

"Listen, you wise guy—" Benny growled as he pushed open the door. "I've taken about enough of your meddling. You're going to get it now!"

He drove a vicious right to Frank's jaw, but the boy dodged and the blow whistled through the air! He stepped inside a wild swing from Benny's left so that it carried harmlessly over his shoulder.

Then Frank staggered his adversary with a smashing right jab to the solar plexus. As Benny doubled over, Frank caught him with a well-timed left hook to the chin! Dazed, the bully fell to the snow.

"Attaboy, Frank!" Joe cried as he took in the short-lived battle through blinking, watering eyes. "That's the way to handle a sneak!"

"Now get the book, Joe," Frank said as he stood over the beaten Benny.

Tass said nothing as he watched Joe retrieve the yearbook. Then, using some sand from their trunk, the Hardys put Benny's car back on the road. He still glowered at them as they drove off.

Eager to get started on the processing of the burnt record book, Frank and Joe returned home, ate a quick lunch, and then hurried into the workshop over the garage. After several hours the boys had failed to find a chemical combination which would restore the printing on the charred pages. Disappointed, they were roused from their work by heavy footsteps on the stairs. Chet and Callie appeared in the doorway.

"We forgot all about the sleigh ride," Joe groaned as he looked around at the half-completed work. "It must be six o'clock."

"Frank Hardy"—Callie shook her finger in mock anger—"you have a date!"

Frank winked at his brother. "What do you think, Joe? Can we give up our sleuthing for a few hours?"

"Let's go!" Joe grinned. "This problem will still be here for us tomorrow!"

In a few minutes the boys had cleaned up the lab and put on their jackets and boots. Then, with Chet and Callie, they hurried out to the waiting sleigh. Climbing aboard, the Hardys were greeted heartily by Iola and half a dozen other friends who made up the party.

With the happy group snuggled in the deep

"That's the way to handle a sneak!" Joe cried

straw, old Mr. Kemper flicked the reins and the two horses broke into a trot. Smoothly the sleigh glided along and for half an hour the crisp night air echoed with the laughter and joking of the young people.

Suddenly Frank and Joe noticed that Mr. Kemper was heading the sleigh toward Woodson Academy.

"Say," Joe whispered excitedly to his brother, "we're not far from the camping hut. Wonder if there's any activity there tonight?"

"You mean—by the Yellow Feather?"

"Yes. We could take a swing over that way and investigate," Joe suggested eagerly.

"What *is* this about investigating yellow feathers?" Callie demanded.

"It's *the* Yellow Feather," Joe said. "Somebody we'd like to catch—and he might be right around here, too."

By this time everyone in the party was listening to the conversation with avid interest.

"Of course we might not find anything at all," Frank murmured to Joe as they neared the place.

For answer, Joe gripped his brother's arm and pointed as the hut came into view.

"Frank! There's a light inside. Someone *is* there!"

CHAPTER XV

A Frightened Bully

"WE'D better stop here," Frank called to Mr. Kemper. "I don't want to get so close to the hut that we'll be heard."

When the driver had reined in, Frank vaulted from the sleigh, landing noiselessly in the snow.

"Joe! Chet! We'd better go the remainder of the way on foot," he whispered. "The rest of you stay here, and please be as quiet as possible."

Thrilled to see the Hardys in action, their friends promised to remain still. They sat in the sleigh and watched in the moonlight as Frank, Joe, and Chet moved off among the trees in the direction of the light.

Soundlessly the trio crept up to the building. Flattening themselves against the stonework below one of the windows, they listened. Two people were evidently arguing.

Henry Kurt and Benny Tass!

"Listen here," Kurt ordered. "You go back and get that book or there'll be trouble. And this time no excuses!"

"But how?" Benny whined. "The Hardy boys have probably warned their family not to give it to me."

"How dumb can you be?" Kurt snorted in disgust. "I said, get that yearbook!"

"You mean you want me to break into their house?" Benny asked in disbelief.

"All I'm telling you," Kurt said in a chilling tone, "is to get that book back before the Yellow Feather catches up with you!"

There were footsteps across the floor and the squeaking of a door.

"Step back!" Frank warned Joe and Chet.

The door opened and Benny Tass came out, his head hanging, his shoulders slumped. In the doorway stood Kurt.

"Remember what I told you," he said in a cold, impersonal voice. "It'll make a difference in your school marks and your scholarship!"

Then the door slammed, and Benny dragged himself off.

"Go after him!" Frank whispered to Joe and Chet. "I'll keep an eye on Kurt."

Stealthily the two followed the bully into the woods. When Joe and Chet were out of earshot of the cabin, Joe called out:

"Benny! Wait for us!"

Tass whirled around. "Wh-what are you guys doing here?" he gasped.

"We happened to be going by with some friends," Joe told him. "When we saw a light in the cabin, we thought we'd do a little investigating."

Benny was frightened. "Did you hear what Kurt said in there?" he asked.

"Part of it."

"The part about the Yellow Feather—and getting the yearbook back?"

The boys nodded, and Joe asked, "Can't you see Kurt's just using you? And you're taking a chance on going to jail!"

"Oh, no," Benny cried in alarm.

"How'd you get mixed up with Kurt?" Joe demanded.

"I wanted to solve the case," came the startling answer. "I thought I could beat you fellows."

Now Benny spilled the whole story, eager to confide in someone.

"Kurt told me about the mystery before you guys ever showed up. He said that I could help in return for the scholarship. I thought I was going to catch the Yellow Feather myself, until you Hardys came along. When I heard that Greg Woodson asked you up to his room, I fixed that wire in the hallway so I could listen without being caught."

Joe clenched his fists and flushed with anger,

but realized he must remain calm to get more information out of Benny.

"Were you the one who was using the ladder to climb into our room?"

"Yes. I planned to play a gag on you that would scare you off the case," Benny admitted sheepishly. "But something happened to the ladder, and I took a mean flop. I got in your room later, but because I was seen by one of the fellows I couldn't do what I planned. So I just took your brother's pants and threw them on the tower."

"Someone pulled the ladder away," Joe said. "You don't know who it was?"

"No."

Chet looked at him sternly. "Did you have anything to do with knocking me out in the tool house and painting a yellow feather on the side of it?"

Benny looked frightened. "No! Outside of what I've told you, the only thing I did was try to shove the Hardys off the road one night. Kurt was with me and suggested it."

"Well, are you going to wise up now and quit being a stooge for Kurt?" Joe asked.

"I don't know. I'm getting sick and tired of having Kurt push me around."

"How would you like to help us instead of him?" Joe suggested. "First of all, have you any idea who the Yellow Feather is?"

"I don't know exactly, but he's somebody

under twenty-one years of age, I guess, from what Kurt once said about him. At least, Kurt once made a crack about the Yellow Feather being a minor.

"Anyway," Benny went on, "the Yellow Feather's someone who has it in for the Woodson family."

"Go ahead," Joe prodded. "What else can you tell us?"

The youth declared that he had told everything he knew about the mysterious enemy. Finally, at the urging of Joe and Chet, Benny agreed to work with them, and if Kurt became too tough on him, to come to them for assistance. He promised to go back to the Academy at once and retire for the night. After he was out of sight, Chet remarked:

"I really think Benny will be all right from now on, Joe."

"If so, it'll be a relief," Joe answered. "And there'll be one less obstacle to overcome."

"Say," said Chet, "what did you think about his information on the Yellow Feather? Could this mysterious guy be a former student at the Academy? A crank who's been holding a grudge?"

"Could be," Joe agreed as both boys cautiously headed for the hut.

Frank, meanwhile, had been spying on the headmaster. When Kurt had closed the door, the young detective had crawled under one of the windows. Now his eyes were on a level with the sill.

The hut was lit by a kerosene lantern. Kurt stood at the table in the center of the room, his back to the boy. He seemed to be studying some papers. Suddenly he turned halfway, holding one up so he could see better.

It was a sheet of white letter paper with rectangular cutouts!

As Frank watched, his heart pounding, Kurt placed the cutout sheet on the table. Then, with a sweep of his hands, he collected all of the other papers into one batch and dropped them into the fireplace. A flick of a match, and they were ablaze.

"What is he up to?" Frank asked himself as Kurt again picked up the cutout sheet and approached the fireplace.

Would he burn it, too?

CHAPTER XVI

An Unexpected Twist

BUT burning the cutout sheet was not Kurt's intention.

As Frank watched, breathless with excitement, the headmaster raised the top of the mantelpiece with one hand. With the other he carefully tucked the paper beneath the lid and closed it. Then he turned out the kerosene lantern.

Backing away from the window, Frank nearly ran into Joe and Chet as they came up behind him. With a motion of his hand, he stilled the questions on their lips. A second later Henry Kurt emerged from the hut and strode off into the darkness.

"Stand guard, will you?" Frank hissed to the others as he moved forward. "I'm going in!"

He opened the door and raced across the room to the fireplace. Stomping with his heavy snow boots on what remained of the flames, he snuffed them out, then recovered what he could of the papers. Relighting the lantern, he studied the scraps.

Apparently they had been torn from many kinds of large-page books, covering a variety of subjects with no significant relationships. There was only one similarity in the sheets—they were all exactly the same size.

"Kurt was probably trying to fit that cutout page over them," the young sleuth deduced. "And since he tossed them all into the fire, none of them could have been the one he was looking for."

Nevertheless, Frank spread the salvaged papers on the table. Then he reached into the space under the movable mantelshelf and pulled out the sheet Kurt had hidden there. The name Hardy was printed in the top left corner.

Was this the original sheet Greg had lost? There was no telling. Only Greg could answer that question.

But as Frank studied it, he noted that the size of the rectangular cutouts and the spacing between them were different from those in the other two sheets he had worked on with Greg.

"All that time spent in the Academy library for nothing," the boy thought ruefully.

At that moment Joe burst impatiently through the hut doorway. "What's going on?" he cried.

Learning that Chet was still on guard, Frank

quickly explained all that he had seen through the window and what he had just found. Joe carefully examined the cutout paper. Then he held it up to the light.

"Say, here's a mark that wasn't on the copy Kurt gave Dad," Joe said.

Scratched on the paper, evidently with a fingernail, and visible only when looked at against the light were two letters: EW.

Elias Woodson!

"This is the real thing!" Frank exclaimed excitedly. "Kurt must have found it the night Greg lost it."

"He has done us a great favor without meaning to," Joe said with a grin. "We'll take this along."

"And leave a fake copy here," said Frank, "so Kurt won't be suspicious."

The Hardys examined the papers Frank had rescued from the fireplace and found an undamaged blank page.

Joe took out his pocketknife and carefully marked small rectangles, then gently punched them out. In a few minutes the job was done. He added the name Hardy and rubbed his hands back and forth over it several times to give the paper a slightly mussed-up appearance, then handed it to Frank.

"Perfect!" his brother said.

He folded the sheet in exactly the same way that the original had been creased. Lifting the top of the mantelshelf, he inserted the fake document.

Then Frank threw the rest of the odd papers into the fireplace and burned them. "Kurt will never know anyone was here," he said.

"Unless Benny Tass tells him!" Joe remarked. He reported the talk with the bully.

"Maybe Benny will reform," Frank said hopefully. "Well, we'll soon know. In any case, we have the lost paper."

After putting the precious sheet into an inside pocket of his jacket, he led the way outside.

When Chet was told of the discovery he whistled gleefully.

"Looks like things are closing in on our friend Kurt," he chortled.

The three boys trudged through the snow to where their friends still waited in Mr. Kemper's sleigh.

"Why, we expected to see you leading a gang of handcuffed prisoners!" Iola teased them.

"You didn't even bring one little crook?" Callie sighed as the sleigh ride got under way again.

Mr. Kemper, as previously arranged, drove to an old inn owned by relatives of one of the girls. The young people spent a fun-filled evening, relishing the fine food for which the place was famous and singing and dancing to the latest records.

The Hardys thoroughly enjoyed every minute of it, but as soon as they returned to Bayport and the quiet of their room, they again discussed the subject foremost in their minds.

"I meant to tell you," Joe reported, "that Benny says Kurt knows who the Yellow Feather is."

"What!"

Joe repeated Tass's theory that the Yellow Feather must be under twenty-one years of age, because Kurt had once spoken of him as being a minor.

"A minor?" Frank puzzled.

"Wait a minute!" Joe cried. "I wonder if Benny misunderstood Kurt. Did he mean *miner* instead of minor—is there a mine mixed up in this case?"

"Elias Woodson may have owned some stock in a mine," Frank mused.

"If the stock has any value, it would be the real reason why the Yellow Feather—and Kurt—are making such a big thing out of the inheritance," Joe observed.

"What kind of mine could it be?" Frank reflected, "and where is it?"

"I think that cutout paper might give us the answer," Joe replied. "I'd like to get to work on it now, but I suppose we'd better get some sleep."

He flipped off the light switch, then moved to

the window to open it for the night. As he did, a vague shifting of shadows below caught his attention.

Joe stared at the moonlit scene outside. Not one, but two figures were moving in the dark protection of the trees and hedges.

He called to Frank, who was out of bed and at his side in an instant. One figure was close to the house now, almost under their window. The other seemed to be following him.

"Out the back door!" Frank suggested.

In a flash, the boys were rushing barefoot down the back stairs.

"Joe, I'll sneak out and get the second guy," Frank said. "When you see me tackle him, snap on the porch light and nab the first one!"

"Okay."

They opened the door silently and Frank padded softly along the edge of the back porch in the shadows, while Joe stood poised with his hand on the light switch.

A moment later Frank made a headlong tackle for his man. Joe snapped on the light and went after the other!

CHAPTER XVII

A Startling Story

FRANK's slashing tackle crashed the silent figure to the ground. The man rolled with the force of the boy's dive, then bounced to his feet.

"Dad!" Frank cried.

At this outburst, Joe stopped in his tracks and whirled about with a look of incredulity on his face.

"Holy crow!" he said. "What's—?"

"Tell you later!" his father cried. "Joe, get that snooper. Don't let him escape!"

Joe dashed toward the front of the house, where the intruder had fled. Mr. Hardy and Frank followed. But the five-second delay had been enough for the fugitive. He had vanished into the night!

"Let's spread out and search the area," Frank said. But before he had time to race off, his father countermanded the proposal.

"Nothing doing," Mr. Hardy said. "You boys

are shivering. Go into the house. I'll try to trace the prowler alone."

As Frank and Joe went inside they were met by Mrs. Hardy and Aunt Gertrude. Upon learning that the prowler had not entered the house, the boys' mother sighed in relief and said she would fix hot cocoa for them and Mr. Hardy.

Aunt Gertrude, however, burst into a tirade. "Burglar or no burglar," she said sternly to her nephews. "The idea of your running out in pajamas in the middle of the night! And in bare feet!"

By the time the cocoa was ready, Mr. Hardy was back. He reported that the intruder had made a clean getaway. Then he looked at Frank.

"That was a great tackle you made, son."

"I'm sorry, Dad. I was sure you were a prowler."

"How did you happen to be trailing that guy?" Joe asked him.

"I was just coming home," Mr. Hardy answered, "when I saw somebody slip across the hedge at the rear and head for the house. Naturally I followed, and was just about ready to challenge him when Frank hit me."

"It's too bad I picked on the wrong man," Frank said ruefully.

Mrs. Hardy served cocoa and cookies to the entire family. As they ate, Frank and Joe told the others the latest developments in the case—

the chase after Benny and the yearbook, the clue of the miner or minor, and the recovery of the original cutout sheet.

"Tomorrow we'll go back to the Woodson library and start looking again for a clue," Joe said.

"And in Dad's yearbook, too," Frank added.

Suddenly the older detective's eyes lighted up. "Boys," he said, "I believe you've solved this mystery!"

Frank and Joe stared at him in astonishment. "How?" they asked together.

"Let me see that sheet," Mr. Hardy requested. "And bring the yearbook down with you too."

"Sure thing." Frank dashed from the kitchen and ran upstairs for the two objects. In a moment the detective was flipping through the yearbook's pages, with his sons looking over his shoulders. As he paused to gaze at a certain page, the boys saw a picture of Mr. Hardy in a Woodson basketball uniform, and a short account of his prowess on the court.

"I believe," Mr. Hardy went on, "that Elias Woodson's message to Greg is in this article. That's why he printed the name Hardy on the corner of the cutout sheet."

Deftly he placed the sheet of paper over the page. With a pencil he drew sharp black lines around the words and parts of words that were showing. Everyone waited breathlessly to see what the message would be. When Mr. Hardy removed the sheet, the page looked as follows:

FENTON HARDY

Woodson's high-scoring forward set the pace with 26 points to help the Yellow and Black beat Craigly. Another feather in Hardy's cap was the golden opportunity he seized to sink the winning basket that determined the state championship one week later. Man of the year in athletics. To the Bayport Ace and our winning team, congratulations!

Quickly Frank read aloud the special message: " 'Yellow Feather Gold Mine Manitoba.' "

"Then there is a mine—a gold mine in Canada!" Joe cried. "Wait until Greg hears this!"

"Yes, but we must be careful about telling him," Mr. Hardy cautioned both his sons. "One thing I'm sure of. Even if Kurt knows there's a mine, he doesn't know where it is and we don't want him to get any inkling of the location."

"After that prowler's visit—and I believe it might have been Kurt—we'd better lock both the paper and the book in your safe, Dad," Frank advised.

"We'll do it at once," said Mr. Hardy, rising from the kitchen chair. He and the boys went upstairs. "When you tell Greg about the mine," the detective warned them, "be sure there are no eavesdroppers around."

Joe remarked that the easiest way out would be to have Kurt arrested. It was obvious that he was trying to steal the Woodson estate.

"We don't have enough on him yet," Mr. Hardy reminded his son. "I'm just as concerned as you are that he's mixed up in the case for selfish reasons, but we must let him tip his own hand."

"How?"

"Well, I'd guess Kurt is delaying a final move for two reasons. First, he knows about the mine. He probably got that much out of Elias Woodson. But as I said, he doesn't know where it is. And secondly," the investigator pointed out, "he must find the old man's will and destroy it. Then, when there's no danger that someone else will inherit the property, Kurt will produce a forged will, leaving everything to him, and pretend it has just been found."

The three discussed means of foiling Kurt's evil scheme. Mr. Hardy decided the best thing for him to do was fly to Manitoba and look for the mine.

"There must be some record of ownership which could be produced in court. In the meantime, you try to get some more information on Kurt's relationship with this Dilleau," the detective suggested as the discussion broke up for the night.

By the time the boys arose the next morning, Mr. Hardy had left for Manitoba on an early plane.

"We'd better get back to work on restoring that article about Dilleau," Frank said to Joe.

As soon as breakfast was over, he and Joe headed for their laboratory in the garage loft. Picking up the experiments that had been interrupted the night before, they again subjected the charred remains of the papers to various chemicals. Finally they found the right combination.

"Look—some of the printing is reappearing!" Joe exulted.

Bit by bit, most of the material on Harris Dilleau became legible. The article had been published in one of the monthly school bulletins.

"Dilleau was president of the school's Science Club," Frank remarked. "And here it says he had a touch of genius. That's why he got such terrific grades in all the sciences," Joe added.

Just then they heard Aunt Gertrude calling them to the telephone.

"I'll take it," Frank offered and hurried to the house. Returning a few minutes later, he said, "It was Chet."

"What did he want?"

"Asked us to help him put some kind of reverse gear on that propeller sled," Frank explained. "But I told him we were going right back to the Academy and he offered to drive us out there in his jalopy."

"Swell, only I hope it gets us there."

Chet arrived fifteen minutes later. Squeezed in the front seat with the stout youth, Frank and Joe clung to the dashboard of the topless car to steady themselves. Between the jouncing and the racket, conversation was impossible.

When they reached the Academy, the Hardys hopped out, thanked Chet, and hurried into the main building. First they checked on the whereabouts of the headmaster and learned from Mr. Teevan that Kurt had taken a party of younger boys some distance into the woods to build a snow fort. Benny Tass, too, was out of the building. Frank and Joe went upstairs to see if Greg was in his room.

"We can talk to him without having Kurt or Benny spying on us," Joe remarked.

Fortunately, Greg was there. When informed of the discovery that the Yellow Feather was a gold mine and not a person, he gasped in amazement.

"If only it's a producing one," he said excitedly, "I'll be able to use the money to put the school back on a paying basis!"

"Take it easy," Frank said, trying to calm their enthusiastic friend. "First we'll have to find your grandfather's will and the deed to the mine. My dad has gone to Manitoba to work on it from that end."

"What's the first move for us?" Greg asked.

"I think we should get in touch with Skinny's uncle—the one who was in Dilleau's class here," Frank suggested. "If we could locate Harris Dilleau, maybe we'd find out why he wanted revenge—"

Luckily, Skinny had not left yet to help with the snow fort. He called his uncle John Mason and after a few words handed the phone to Frank.

"Last I heard about Dilleau," Mr. Mason said, "his name had been added to the list of wanted criminals in his home state."

"Why?"

"He escaped from prison while serving a long term as a swindler. Through some clever invention that had to do with spring propulsion he managed to get out."

"How long ago was that?" Frank questioned, his excitement mounting.

"Oh, about three years. And I read in the paper recently that there hasn't been a trace of him since."

Thanking Mr. Mason for his assistance, Frank hung up and stepped outside the booth. Smiling at Skinny, he said:

"Your uncle was a great help. I guess that's

all we need now. Don't you want to go out and help with the snow fort?"

"Yes, I do," Skinny replied. "So long, fellows."

After Skinny had gone, Frank repeated the phone conversation to Joe and Greg, and added:

"I'm sure now that Harris Dilleau and Henry Kurt are the same person!"

CHAPTER XVIII

Cannonballs of Ice

GREG's face registered shock. "You mean a hunted criminal is running this school?"

"There are several reasons that point to it," Frank said. "First, we know that Kurt has a flair for inventing things."

"And so did Dilleau," Joe burst out. "That yearbook mentioned that he was head of the Science Club."

"But what about school pictures of him around here?" Greg asked. "Even though he's older, it wouldn't be too hard to identify him and no one ever has."

"The night after you and Frank discovered Kurt looking at the desk with Harris D on it," Joe said, "he ordered all the old records burned."

"That's right," Greg conceded. "But I still can't see why my grandfather didn't recognize him."

"All Kurt needed to do in order to hide his identity was to have a plastic surgery job and grow that goatee," Frank pointed out.

Now that the case against Kurt looked so strong, Greg was determined to call in the police. But the Hardys tried to talk him out of a rash move.

"We haven't enough evidence yet," Frank cautioned him.

"Besides," Joe added, "how about the reputation of the school? Every pupil in the place might leave if the authorities came charging in here and caused a lot of unfavorable publicity."

"When Dad gets back," Frank said, "he can arrange that everything be taken care of quietly."

Greg was convinced, but suggested they keep a twenty-four-hour watch on the headmaster. Frank thought this unnecessary. With the will missing, the man would not be likely to leave Woodson.

"But we might go and see what he's doing now. He may be up to something more than directing the building of a snow fort."

Greg put on his heavy boots and jacket, then the three hurried outside. As they rounded the corner of the administration building a husky figure approached them.

"Hi, you guys!" Benny called. "What angles are you working on today?"

Warily Frank glanced at Joe. Had this boy

really turned over a new leaf and joined their side? Frank decided to be sure before revealing any information.

"Nothing much so far," he replied in as friendly a voice as he could manage.

"Where are you heading?" Joe asked, just to make conversation.

"They say that's quite an ice fort the kids are building out in the woods. I thought I might watch them for a while."

Frank, wanting to keep an eye on Benny, suggested that they all walk over together. Deep in the woods, they came upon the nearly finished fort. Set back against a knoll, and surrounded by high trees, it looked unassailable.

"Those walls must be three feet thick," Joe said in amazement as he studied the snow fort.

"It looks more like a giant igloo than the kind of open snow fort we used to build when we were kids," Frank remarked, his attention focused on the vaulted roof which covered the entire structure. The entrance was a narrow slit in one side.

Under Kurt's direction, students were busy carrying buckets back and forth to a nearby stream. Through a hole chopped in the ice, each boy lowered his pail, filled it, and emptied the water on the fort.

"The water freezes almost immediately," Greg

commented as they watched the process. "The fort must be as hard as granite."

"The whole thing is on the grim side. It's not like a play fort and the boys don't seem to be having much fun," Joe said.

"Hey! Look at Kurt!" Benny spoke up. "He's moving up some kind of cannon."

As the Hardys turned, they saw the head-master swing a harpoon gun on its tripod. The Hardys exchanged significant glances, but the students shrieked in delight.

Kurt was loading it with giant icicles! He took dead aim at the side of the fort and fired. There was a twanging sound like that the Hardys had heard the night of their harrowing experience at Rocky Point. One more bit of evidence against the headmaster!

The spearlike weapon rocketed toward the fort and landed on the roof. But the icicle hardly made a dent in the solid exterior.

Again and again, Kurt sent his "ammunition" whistling toward the fort. The giant icicles exploded into tiny, gleaming fragments as they hit.

Although several students asked to shoot off the gun, Kurt would not permit this. Soon he ordered the whole group back to the Academy and walked off.

"But we haven't had a snowball fight," Skinny objected. "You promised—"

"It's too late," the headmaster replied sternly. "Your lunch will be ready. Hurry now, all of you!"

Disappointed, the boys marched sullenly back to the school. Frank and Joe, together with Greg and Benny, went to inspect the fort at close range.

"Can you imagine being trapped in a thing like this?" Frank asked. "If that door were ever sealed up, anyone inside would be a goner!"

After a complete inspection of the fort, the four headed back to the school. When they reached the main building, Benny said good-by cordially.

"Looks as if reform is really taking hold," Joe commented.

After lunch Greg and the Hardys decided on going directly to the school library since no one would be in it at that time of day.

"This time we *must* find a clue," Greg said. "I'm worried that Kurt will do it ahead of us."

They were halfway up the stairs when a student called to Frank and Joe from below.

"Hey! You Hardys! There's a long-distance telephone call for you. Make it snappy!"

"Dad!" the boys said in unison as they turned and ran down the steps.

Together they squeezed into the hallway booth. Frank picked up the phone.

Mr. Hardy's voice came over the wire clear

and strong. After a quick exchange of greetings, he reported on the work he was doing in Winnipeg.

"I've been talking to authorities up here about the location of the Yellow Feather Mine," he said. "They tell me that there isn't any such operation listed in the province, and no one has ever heard of it."

The boys' hearts sank. They asked him if the mine angle was a dud.

"No, not at all," Mr. Hardy assured them. "I was lucky enough to run into an elderly hotel man up here named Davis. He knew Elias Woodson well. He often stayed at the hotel. Woodson was very fond of this province, it seems. Davis said the old gentleman once told him that he owned a producing gold mine."

"Did he say where it was?" Frank asked eagerly.

"Yes. Colorado. I'm going to fly there and find out what I can."

"When, Dad?"

"I'll leave here in a couple of hours," his father replied. "Now so much for that, son. Mr. Davis gave me another important piece of information. The tower has a secret—"

There was a clicking sound and the connection was suddenly cut off.

CHAPTER XIX

Victory Snatched Away

"HELLO! Hello!" Frank shouted into the mouthpiece. "I was cut off, operator!"

But though she tried, the operator could not restore Mr. Hardy's connection from Winnipeg.

"Sorry," she said, and Frank hung up.

"I wonder what Dad was going to tell us," Joe pondered.

"All I could get was that the bell tower has some kind of secret," Frank murmured in disappointment. "Perhaps a hidden room."

"Well, what are we waiting for? Come on. Let's investigate and find out," Joe said eagerly.

It was arranged that Greg would keep tabs on the headmaster during the search. Kurt had locked himself in his office and did not reappear for a long while.

In the meantime, the Hardys went to the catwalk of the tower and looked at the exterior of the structure. From his former trip to the belfry, Joe knew there was no visible entrance.

But there might be a concealed one.

"Surely when the original stairway was removed," he said, "some means of entrance must have been substituted."

Every inch of the belfry wall was tapped. Frank even stood on Joe's shoulders to investigate in order not to miss any possibility.

"No go," he said finally. "If there's an entrance, it's somewhere inside. Maybe in the attic where the bell tower joins the roof."

For the first time the boys realized that the architecture of the school was a bit odd. The belfry was located where one wing joined the main part of the building.

"I think," said Frank, "that once upon a time the tower extended up on the outside of the main building and the wing was constructed around it."

"Then the thing to do is examine the tower where it passes through each floor," Joe said.

The boys hurried to the basement, where the foundation of the circular structure was plainly visible. But the section where a door into it had once been was solidly bricked in with a lighter shade of mortar.

The boys went to the main floor and marveled at the clever way the architect had covered up any evidence of the former tower. A series of cabinets and shelves hid the old structure.

"No entrance here," Frank muttered and started for the stairway.

The room adjoining the old tower shaft on the second floor was a large study hall, now vacant. The room was pine-paneled, whereas the other rooms had plastered walls.

"I'll bet there's a secret panel here!" Frank cried. "Keep watch in the hall, Joe, while I do some tapping."

Inch by inch, Frank used his knuckles and fingertips on the wood. There were hollow and solid sounds but nothing moved or even vibrated. He tried pushing sideways against the trim that covered the seams between the pine boards.

Suddenly a section of the wall began to move!

"Joe! S-s-st!"

His brother came on the run and had to stifle a shout of glee when he saw the opening. Frank said he was going inside. In the event that he could not get out, Joe was to open the door when Frank tapped on the panel.

"Give me ten minutes," Frank suggested and closed himself in.

Joe ambled back to the hall. To his consternation, Greg and Kurt were coming up the nearest stairway together. Joe walked toward them, pretending to be on his way down.

With a bare nod, Kurt brushed past him.

The wall began to move!

Then, stiffly saying "Good-by" to Greg, the headmaster turned into the study hall.

Joe was aghast. He must get Kurt out of there at once! Frank might tap on the panel at any moment! He motioned to Greg to wait.

"Oh, Mr. Kurt," he said, racing back, "my brother and I made an interesting discovery today. Won't you come down to the guest room? I'd like to show it to you."

All this time Joe was trying to figure out just what to show Kurt which would keep the headmaster occupied while he returned to let Frank out. It would even be better if Greg went back to do it.

"I'm very busy," said Kurt, "but I'll go."

When the three reached the room, Joe had decided what to tell the headmaster. His back to Kurt, he noisily riffled some newspapers in the bureau drawer. But he also was scribbling a note to Greg on the top border of one of them.

"Where is that clipping?" he said aloud as he wrote:

> *Tower end of study hall. Push third panel from left. Let Frank out.*

After quickly tearing off the note and wadding it, Joe gave the newspapers a final rattle, then turned around.

"Mr. Kurt, I'm afraid your cleaning woman tidied up altogether too well. But," he added, passing in front of Greg and pushing the note into his hand, "if you can spare a few more minutes, I'll tell you the gist of what we discovered."

Greg arose. "Guess you two don't need me. I have to make a phone call," he said.

When he had left, Joe said slowly and with great emphasis, "We saw a printed article that gave us an idea. There's a gold mine named the Yellow Feather!"

Kurt jumped out of the chair on which he had been waiting impatiently, his face ash white.

"You—you— Where did you see that?" he demanded. "A newspaper? Let me see it at once. Oh, you said the cleaning woman had thrown it out. I'll look in the trash. I'll—"

Still muttering incoherently, the headmaster made a beeline for the stairway and disappeared. Joe chuckled softly.

"I didn't say we saw the notice in a *newspaper,* you moneygrubber," he murmured.

Meanwhile, Frank had made a startling discovery in the tower's second-floor room which was completely cut off from the lower section. Near the door lay the discarded desk top with the ominous carved words: REVENGE HARRIS D.

Using his pocket flashlight, Frank noticed similar messages on the underside. I HATE WOODSON. IT WILL SUFFER SOMEDAY. DILLEAU.

"I see why Kurt wanted to hide this desk top,"

Frank thought as he beamed the light around the circular room.

There were various sorts of propulsion gadgets and other sinister-looking objects—no doubt inventions of Kurt. In the pulled-out drawers of an old-fashioned bureau lay a pile of small yellow feathers and a supply of wigs, false beards and mustaches.

Frank nearly laughed aloud. "I wonder if Kurt's goatee is real," he thought.

A winding staircase led to the roof. Frank climbed it gingerly, but there was nothing at the top except a weatherproof ventilator. Frank spent the rest of the time looking for the will but did not find it. At the end of the ten-minute period he returned to the panel to wait for Joe to let him out. Though Frank was sure he could open it, he did not want to be discovered coming through the secret door.

As he waited, the door suddenly slid back, revealing Greg. "I'll explain everything in a minute," he whispered as Frank stepped through and closed the panel. "Hurry!"

Frank followed and they met Joe in the hall.

"Where's Kurt?" Greg whispered.

"In the cellar. Let's go talk outdoors where he can't bother us."

The three took a long walk where they could laugh without restraint at the trick Joe had played on Kurt. But finally they became serious, and after Frank reported that he had not found the missing will, the conversation got around to the various unsolved angles of the mystery.

"I have a hunch if we could figure out the meaning of that word *Manitoba*—" Joe said slowly.

But no new ideas occurred to the boys and they returned to the school just as the dinner bell rang.

During the meal the Hardys caught Kurt glancing suspiciously at them several times. Did he suspect their ruse?

"We'd better act pretty nonchalant until we shove off for bed," Frank advised.

They remained with the students during the rest of the evening, then went to their room. When the dorm grew quiet and it was apparent that everyone else was asleep, the Hardys talked in whispers about the mysterious connection between Manitoba and the Yellow Feather case.

"If the mine isn't up there," Joe said, "I don't understand why old Elias would have emphasized the word in that message."

"Unless it was a connecting link to the next clue." Frank sat up straight in his chair. "You don't suppose—the library! Come on, Joe!"

The boys grabbed their sweaters and Frank led the way on tiptoe down the dimly lighted corridor. Once inside the library he turned on his flashlight.

"We're going to look in every book with the word Manitoba in it!"

"Good hunch, Frank. Let's start with the encyclopedia."

"It might be just a word that's circled, or something like that," Frank suggested as they began.

Several editions of encyclopedias, however, failed to yield a single clue. Next, they started on the geographies.

Finishing one stack of books, Joe began to replace them while Frank looked for other possible resources.

"Funny, all these books certainly seemed to be lined up pretty evenly before," Joe grunted as he put the last one back into the case, "but now some of them stick out. Oh, for Pete's sake! No wonder—there's another book behind them."

Reaching in, he pulled out a much older volume, dusty and worn. He was about to shove it into place properly when its title caught his eye.

"Frank! Here's one—*Canada: Province by Province.*"

Joe laid the old volume on the table and flashed the light directly on it as he flipped the book open. As if by magic the heading *Manitoba* stared at them.

And there inserted between the pages was

an old, once-white but now yellowed envelope!

With fingers shaking from excitement, Frank picked it out of the book. Joe held the flashlight close as his brother pulled back the unsealed flap. The legal document within was unfolded. The boys gasped.

" '*The Last Will and Testament*,' " read Joe in a husky whisper, " '*of Elias Woodson!*' "

"We've found it!" Frank whispered exultantly.

Placing the document on the table with the light close above it, they eagerly scanned the legal terminology.

" 'To my nephew, Gregory Woodson,' " Frank read, " 'I give and bequeath my full estate including the Woodson Academy, grounds, buildings, and institution, and the Yellow Feather Gold Mine in Colorado.' "

"Greg gets it all!" Joe cheered as loud as he dared, while Frank checked quickly through the rest of the will.

Both boys were so excited about Greg Woodson's good fortune that neither of them heard the slight shifting of feet behind them. Without warning a voice hissed in their ears:

"Oh, no, he doesn't! But thanks for solving the mystery!"

Henry Kurt!

As the boys spun around to confront the man they felt a fine spray cover their faces. The next instant, Frank and Joe sank to the floor!

Some time later, in total darkness, Frank struggled to regain consciousness. Suddenly, wide awake, he sat bolt upright to discover that he was lying on hard ground!

It was freezing cold. Shivering and chattering, Frank got to his feet. Now he remembered the voice in the library and the thin, fine spray that had hit him and Joe in the face.

"Joe!" he muttered weakly. "Where's Joe?"

As if in answer, his toe hit something soft. Kneeling in the blackness, he found a figure.

"Joe!"

"What happened?" Joe asked dazedly.

Tersely, Frank reminded him of the whispered threat in the library and the spray that apparently had knocked them both out.

"But where are we?" Joe asked weakly.

"I have no idea," Frank replied. It was so black that he could not even see his brother's face.

When Joe had revived enough to stand, they began to feel their way around the place where they were confined. All they found was a rough, hard, cold wall enclosing them. A horrible realization began to dawn on Frank.

"We're sealed inside Kurt's ice fort!"

CHAPTER XX

The Final Roundup

"WE'LL never escape!" Joe's cry echoed in the tomblike enclosure.

Because the boys had inspected the fort so carefully only that day, they knew it would be impossible to claw their way through those three-foot walls of solid ice. Kurt had done his evil work well.

Suddenly it occurred to Frank that there was one possible means of escape. "The entrance! It can't be frozen as hard as the rest of the wall—not yet, anyway!"

It was their only hope. On hands and knees the young detectives circled their small prison until they found an indentation indicating the doorway.

"Good thing he didn't pack this as thick as the rest of the wall," Frank chattered.

With numbed hands, and using Joe's pocketknife they took turns digging at the rock-hard surface. It was torturous work.

They had dug part of a tiny tunnel, little wider than a fist, when the knife suddenly penetrated the last bit of outside wall.

"We're through!" Joe exulted. "And it's morning."

Desperately Frank scraped until he had enlarged the small opening. A blast of fresh air came whistling through.

"We may freeze, but we won't suffocate," Joe muttered.

"Maybe we can make a hole large enough to squeeze through," Frank said hopefully.

Their joy was short-lived; for, just as Frank started to dig again, the pocketknife blade snapped in two! Its other blades were too small to be of any use.

"The only thing we can do now is shout, and hope someone hears us," Frank declared.

Taking turns, they began to yell for help through the narrow opening. There was no reply.

Back at the school, at this very moment, Greg was talking on the telephone. He was worried and excited.

"Hello, Chet?" he cried into the mouthpiece. "You'd better come out here, quick! The Hardys have disappeared. . . . I don't know. I woke up early and saw Kurt sneaking back into the school. It was shortly after dawn. He had no reason to be out at that hour. I suspect something's up."

Greg hung up and put on his outdoor clothes.

Where could the Hardys be? The question ran round and round in Greg's mind while he impatiently awaited Chet. Finally the boy arrived in his father's farm truck.

"I borrowed this," Chet yelled, "so I could bring my propeller sled. We can cover more ground on it."

They lifted off the sled and Chet started the motor while Greg parked the truck.

"Where do we go first?" Chet asked.

"Let's try the woods," Greg suggested, running back and jumping on the sled.

As they bounced along one of the trails, Chet noticed the ice fort. "What's that?" he asked.

"Something Kurt had the fellows build yesterday. Oh, good night, the doorway's sealed up!" Greg cried as they neared the fort. "It had an opening yesterday! You don't suppose—"

"Looks as if someone has cut a small hole through the wall," Chet remarked as he stopped the sled. He hopped off, placed his mouth near the opening, and shouted:

"Frank! Joe! Hey, anybody inside?"

There was no answer.

"We must break through that wall!" Greg cried. "We'll get picks and crowbars."

"And waste too much time," Chet said. "If Frank and Joe are in there, we must get them out pronto!"

"But how?"

"I have it!" Chet announced. "I spent all day yesterday fixing this gimmick. Look out!"

Bouncing back onto the propeller sled, he put the gears into reverse. Then hastily he backed the sled to the wall of the fort. With the propellers spinning so that their sharp edges cut into the hard ice, he backed the sled against the wall.

"It's biting the ice away!" Greg cried.

Chunks and fragments of ice flew in all directions. Suddenly the last of the barrier gave way, and Chet had to kill the engine at once so that the sled would not push right into the enclosure.

Greg was already peering inside. Two figures lay motionless on the ground.

"Frank and Joe!" he exclaimed, terror in his voice.

Chet looked at his friends' still bodies a second, then sprang into action.

"Come on, Greg. Give me a hand!"

The Hardys were carried out into the pale warmth of the winter morning sun. Frank and Joe were still breathing. With Greg and Chet giving first aid, they quickly recovered consciousness. Feebly Frank murmured:

"Have Kurt arrested!"

"You go ahead and take care of that, Greg," Chet ordered. "I'll bring the boys. It'll have to be a slow, easy ride."

Greg waited long enough to help bundle Frank and Joe aboard the sled, then he raced off on foot. Halfway to the school he met Benny Tass.

"What's the big hurry?" the boy asked.

Forgetting that Benny might still be loyal to Kurt, Greg blurted out the story of the near-fatal kidnapping of the Hardys. All the color drained from Benny's face.

"Have you seen Kurt?" Greg demanded.

"A little while ago," Benny answered. "He asked me where you and Chet were going, and I told him you were looking for the Hardys."

"Come on. We're going to his room," Greg commanded.

But the headmaster was not there. Greg called the police, then he and Benny rushed from one end of the school to the other without finding any trace of the missing man. They concluded that he must have realized that things were closing in on him and had fled.

As they abandoned their search, Chet slowly maneuvered the sled to the main entrance. Willing hands helped move the Hardys into the school infirmary. Fortunately, the nurse had returned from her vacation.

"They'll be all right, with some treatment and rest," she told the others.

Before Frank and Joe went to sleep, Greg assured them that the police had been alerted to be on the lookout for Kurt.

By the next morning, neither of the Hardys was any the worse for his harrowing experience, and the police came to take full statements from both boys. Since Kurt had not been found, Frank and Joe insisted upon lending a hand. Besides capturing the criminal, they were determined to recover the will!

As Greg and Chet came to the infirmary door, they met the boys just coming out. In their haste the Hardys ran full tilt into their friends.

"Thought you were sick," Chet gasped, recovering his balance.

"Come on with us!" Joe cried. "We think we know where Kurt is!"

To Chet's and Greg's amazement, they went to the second floor, then disappeared into the study hall. Frank pushed back the secret panel and flashed a light inside the dark room. Everyone peered in.

"Kurt's not here," Joe announced in disappointment.

But Frank's sharp eyes had noticed a pile of rugs which had not been there the day before. Stepping into the room, he lifted the rugs to reveal a crouching figure.

The wily headmaster!

Kurt never had a chance to move. He was surrounded and yanked to his feet by the four husky boys. Still defiant, he tried to shake them off, asking what right they had to apprehend him.

"You answer that," Frank said.

As he stabbed a hand into the man's inside coat pocket Kurt struggled and cursed.

"The will!" Frank cried gleefully as he retrieved the envelope. Handing it to Greg, he said, "Your grandfather left his entire estate to you!"

Greg was too dumbfounded to speak. Joe told him how they had found the document, only to have it snatched from them.

"How can I ever repay you?" the happy heir cried. "Money could never make up for risking your lives to help me."

The Hardys smiled. "Don't try," Frank said. "We like catching criminals."

Kurt, completely beaten, confessed everything Frank and Joe had suspected about his nefarious efforts to deprive Greg of his rightful inheritance.

In desperation he had had the ice fort built, hoping to imprison the young detectives.

"I'm Dilleau," he admitted. "When I was a student here, I was caught stealing. Elias Woodson gave me a tongue-lashing, for which I have hated him ever since. I determined to get revenge and tried to sell some of his valuable books, but he found me out and I was expelled."

Kurt went on to say that he had planned for

years to come back and be headmaster—maybe even succeed in taking the school away from its owner. But, in the meantime, he had run afoul of the law and had spent some time in prison.

"I escaped," the man explained. "Then I had my face operated on and grew this goatee. When I came back here, Woodson didn't recognize me. I showed him some phony papers and sold him the idea of giving me the job of assistant headmaster. I had a lot of theatrical gear and used to disguise myself to do a little thievery.

"Old man Woodson made the mistake of telling me about that gold mine and I resolved to get hold of it. One evening I saw his will and knew I would have to destroy it. But Mr. Woodson was clever—he took the will out of his desk and hid it."

Kurt then told how, shortly before Woodson's death, the old man told him he was devising a puzzle so that no one could steal the estate from his grandson.

"Maybe he suspected me," Kurt said, then went on, "I surprised Woodson in the library making a sheet with cutouts. Just then a student called me. When I got back, the paper was gone and the old man was lying in a faint. He died the next day."

"And you found the cutout sheet on the river?" Frank asked him.

"Yes. I thought it would throw your father

and everyone else off the track if I made a fake one and said Mr. Woodson had given it to me."

Presently plainclothesmen came to arrest Kurt. They planned to keep him at Bayport headquarters until the authorities of the prison from which he had escaped arrived to take charge.

Chet was sure nothing so exciting would ever happen again, but he and the Hardys soon became involved in another thrilling adventure, *The Hooded Hawk Mystery*.

Since Benny Tass and Skinny Mason already knew so much about the case, they were told the details.

"Kurt was the one who knocked Joe out at the hut while you were asleep, Benny," Frank said. "He waited until my brother went outside for wood, then slugged him, hid his skis and dragged him off to the boathouse before you woke up. He also conked me near the Teevans' cottage, with Benny's help."

As Benny, conscience-stricken, looked down at the floor, Greg took up the story. "Kurt was the one who put the poison in my coffee and then stuck a yellow feather under the cup. Needless to say, he never reported the incident to the police."

Benny became more ashamed. "To think I fell for that stuff about the Yellow Feather being a person!" he groaned.

"We all did," Greg said.

Young Woodson told Benny that he was convinced Kurt's warped sense of humor was partly responsible. The headmaster had apparently enjoyed leading him on about the Yellow Feather and the play on the words *miner* and *minor*.

"Another one of his jokes," Frank stated, "was jimmying the lock on his own office door and planting my scarf there."

"Kurt probably hastened my grandfather's death with exaggerations about the bad financial conditions here at the school," Greg remarked. "And he tried to scare me off with a lot of phony threats."

"But how about the time Chet was knocked out in the tool shed?" Benny inquired.

"Kurt did that, too," Frank replied, "with a dart from one of his propulsion guns. And he fired harpoons at us from Rocky Point."

"And remember the time we got the yearbook back from you," Joe could not resist needling Tass. "That same night Kurt was prowling around our house. Dad barely missed catching him."

"I'm sorry I ever got mixed up with him," Benny said. "I've learned my lesson, fellows. Say, I wonder if Kurt was the one who tipped that ladder the night I started to climb to your room."

"No," said a voice familiar to the Hardy boys. They turned to see their father standing in the doorway. "As a matter of fact," Mr. Hardy went on, "I was the one."

Grinning, the famous detective told Benny that for a few minutes he had thought the ladder climber was the Yellow Feather.

"Me!" Benny exclaimed.

Frank introduced his father to Greg Woodson, who thanked him and his sons for their clever detective work.

Mr. Hardy smiled. "The case was an unusual one. Coming back to my old school to work on a mystery and learning that a secret entrance to the tower had been built was exciting in itself." He turned to Frank and Joe. "Mr. Woodson's old friend in Winnipeg told me this. I was afraid the Yellow Feather might imprison one of you in the tower."

He suddenly laughed heartily. "Do you know," he added, "this is the first time a criminal ever came to me as Kurt did and asked me to help him catch himself!"

"So there wasn't really any Yellow Feather after all," Chet spoke up.

"Except the mine," the detective said. "And, Greg, there's plenty of gold left!"

Greg's eyes glistened. "I'll go out there after graduation. Want to come along, fellows?"

There was a chorus of "Do we!"

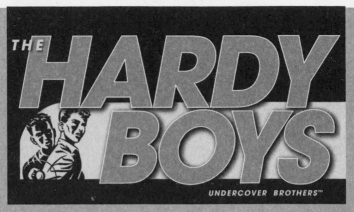

THE HARDY BOYS

UNDERCOVER BROTHERS™

THIS MISSION REQUIRES YOUR IMMEDIATE ATTENTION.

Read Frank and Joe's latest stories of crime, danger, mystery, and death-defying stunts!

  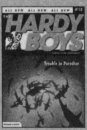

BLOWN AWAY   HURRICANE JOE   TROUBLE IN PARADISE

THE MUMMY'S CURSE   HAZED

Visit www.SimonSaysSleuth.com for a complete list of Hardy Boys titles.

ALADDIN PAPERBACKS • SIMON & SCHUSTER CHILDREN'S PUBLISHING • A CBS COMPANY

The Hardy Boys © Simon & Schuster, Inc.

Match Wits with The Hardy Boys®!

Collect the Complete
Hardy Boys Mystery Stories®
by Franklin W. Dixon

The Hardy Boys Back-to-Back

Celebrate over 70 Years with the World's Greatest Super Sleuths!

Match Wits with Super Sleuth Nancy Drew!

Collect the Complete
Nancy Drew Mystery Stories®
by Carolyn Keene

Celebrate over 70 years with the World's Best Detective!